Collection of Short Stories

Jim Seckler

ACKNOWLEDGMENTS

I regret the education I disregarded, squandered and finally discovered a little late in life. But better late than never, I guess. All of the problems of the world can be solved with a healthy dose of education.

CONTENTS

THE PIER

My knees hurt. Whenever that happened, something bad, something scary was about to happen. I didn't know what, but I expected my life would change forever.

The cool wind blew off the choppy Pacific Ocean lifting a squadron of gray pelicans gently up, then down in unison as they skimmed just above the sea. I leaned heavily on the salt and sun-beaten and sea gull poop plastered railing of the city's pier.

The wind blew the few remaining strands of my thin, silver hair around and plays with my fishing line that arcs down into the emerald green water. I figured with the cut up squid on one hook and a half of an anchovy on the other hook that I'm giving the stupid fish a smorgasbord of choices.

The wind also cleared away the smog that blows in from the large city to the north. It also made my knees hurt. Whenever the temperature dropped or when I walk more than usual, the pain would creep into my joints like an annoying relative.

The end of the pier was the only place where I found peace and solace these days. Someone once called a pier the poor man's yacht. The ocean surrounded me except for a ribbon of old, wooden planks that seem like my lifeline back to the shore.

Many years ago, I watched as twenty-foot waves crashed on top of the pier just about where I'm sitting now. The waves destroyed more than half the pier that day, which everyone blamed on storms generated by El Nino. Now, I look down to watch the swells roll gently past the pilings on its way to shore and the waiting surfers who bob like corks in the water on both sides of the pier.

A young couple strolled by me. They're happy and in love and they have their arms linked around each other to fight off the loneliness. They stopped near me and kiss as if they intentionally planned to rub in the fact that I'm alone and they're not. They walked on, secure in the knowledge that I've had enough of their happiness and affection.

Several minutes later, two boys walked by with poles perched on their shoulders like that 1950s television show of a southern sheriff.

"Catch anything?" one of boys asks.

I shook my head and grumbled something and they look into my bucket of dead chovies.

"That's a big one," the other kid said. They both wore smirks and walked on laughing as if they owned the world.

"Smart asses," I said.

They acted like they don't hear me. I stared at the water. I always seemed to find solace in the ocean. In my youth, I spent most of my waking hours in, on or under the water. The ocean seemed like a mother to me. She engulfed me in her loving embrace, rolling me around in fun. When she got mad, she would knock me down with violent fury, taking me to the edge of exhaustion before realizing I have had enough. She taught me things I never knew about myself. I felt sad and a little guilty when I got out of the water after a swim and I would whisper softly to her that I would return as soon as I can.

Now I'm too old to go swimming. It takes a lot out of me just to walk the pier. All 1,400 feet of it. I'm nowhere near the end of the pier.

Several girls walked by and I watched them with envy. They giggled to themselves and without looking back, they pointed back in my direction. They are wearing the latest fashion in swimwear, string bikinis that barely cover their small breasts. Their skinny asses peaked out from narrow material in the back. The sight of them brings back a long ago memory.

I shook my head and think of the girls of my youth. I dated a lot, none very serious though, except one. When I turned thirty and was still single, I knew that I'd still be alone at sixty. Now, I'm almost seventy-five and still alone.

I turned and looked in the direction of the girls and see that they're coming back this way. I wish that they would leave. One of them looked a little like Lisa. Lisa of so many years ago. The hurt won't go away and it's not all in my knees.

I reeled in the line to check the bait and partly to get my mind off the past. I saw that the bait is gone. The girls passed by me without a sound while I reeled in the line all the way in. I baited the hooks again and drop the line back in the water to wait.

I remember years ago, casting way out there, when I used to fish with my friends. They are dead now or have moved away to some trailer park in Arizona. Once, one of my friends, Jack, cast his line out and hooked a surfer on his wet suit. Recalling this makes me smile as I gaze at today's surfers in the distance.

A man walked by and saw me with my idiot grin and guesses that I'm senile. Maybe I am. I continued to smile at my youth. So what. Screw the present and piss on the future.

I felt a tug on the line and I peek over the railing. Nothing else happens and I sit back down. I looked again at the end of the pier. For some reason it looked as if it is getting closer.

"Catch anything?" a man behind me asked.

I turned around and peer into the sunburned face of a young man. He was wearing a fluorescent blue/green bathing suit and a plain naval blue T-shirt. His accent was unfamiliar.

"Naw. Nothing yet," I said.

"What do you usually catch around here?" he asked.

"Mainly Tom Cod and mackerel. A sand shark now and then," I said. I throw in the bit about the shark, since most inlanders still have nightmares about the movie 'Jaws'.

"Sure is a nice day," he said. He tilted his face up to the sun as if to soak up every last bit of its warmth.

Even though it's a warm day, I still wear a jacket. Not much meat on the old bones anymore.

"Good luck with the fishing," he finally said.

I nod my thanks as he leaves. I must remind him of his father or God forbid, grandfather. I shivered at the thought of him or anyone for that matter being my son or, God forbid, grandson.

Several porpoises surfaced past the end of the pier. They dove, then resurfaced a hundred yards or so further on, all in perfect sync with each other. People at the end of the pier pointed in their direction.

They say that a porpoise is an intelligent animal. When I was younger I often dreamed that I was a porpoise and that I could just swim in the ocean forever. Not a bad life. Swim, look for food and mate once in a while. All I do now is look for food. It's sobering to know that an animal does more with its life than I do. However, when was the last time you saw a seventy-year-old porpoise? He's probably shark poop by now.

The sun was setting now and lies at the angle on the water that creates a hell of a glare. Thank God for polarized sunglasses or my eyes would have dried up and fallen out long ago. Despite the warmth I still felt a chill and bury myself deeper into my jacket.

"Hey, Pops," a voice called out.

I hate being called that. I gave the owner of the voice an icy glare. It's Dinky. He's a little younger than me, but looks a lot younger. He plants himself down in a chair next to me. He doesn't have his fishing gear with him, but he does have the ever-present cooler on wheels full of beer.

They are inseparable those two are. One of the most faithful marriages in history. He would never cheat on his beer by going out and having a coke. That would be the scandal and a messy divorce. The beer would take everything and leave him with a bad taste in his mouth. His wife is just as cold and would also leave a bad taste in his mouth.

They have two kids. The son is a lazy, no-good beach bum, who is currently living off his twenty-two-year-old fourth wife who works as a waitress and will someday get smart and dump him. Dinky's son is the heir to the beer throne. Dinky is always telling me about his idiot son. I met him several times, regretting every minute of it. Dinky's third wife was also a waitress and is now a masseuse. Stupidly doesn't fall far from the tree.

"See the game last night? The Forty-niners cleaned the Rams' clock. Think they'll go all the way?" he said.

"Maybe. The Falcons look tough this year," I said.

I was making small talk. Very small talk.

"Nah. Haven't got a chance. My Forty-niners all the way."

"I thought you liked Dallas?"

"No way, Jose," he said with a shocked expression. He once tried to convince me he was a Cowboy fan, but they aren't doing too well lately. He usually roots for the team that's in first place.

"Where's your pole?" I asked.

"The old bitch must have hidden it somewhere. I couldn't find it. We had another row last night," he said.

I had the misfortune to witness one of their fights. No way, Jose. Never again.

"You're lucky," he said. "No one to put a ball and chain around your neck. Go wherever you want. Do whatever you want."

What do I want to do and where do I want to go? I think to myself.

"Yup. Free as a fricken bird," he added.

Yeah. No one to talk to. No one to chase away the blues.

"Hey. Remember that song by Lynyrd Skynyrd? 'Free Bird'?"

"Yeah. A real classic," I said.

"And you look at these kids today with the blue hair and spikes and their stupid ass crap music," he said.

He shook his head at three teenage boys, who are walking by, wearing punk hairdos.

He doesn't mention that his wife has blue hair and his son once shaved his head into the shape of a question mark. His whole family is a question mark. I think of his family with a grin. Dinky thinks I'm grinning at the teenagers and he shakes his head again.

"Hey Frankie," he yelled at a middle-age man with a huge potbelly and the hairiest back I have ever seen on man or beast.

Somehow they let this ape walk around without a shirt. The gorilla turned and waved in our direction. He's wearing only a bathing suit, much to the chagrin of the civilized world.

If a group of aliens landed on the pier just now, they would encounter in no particular order; the blue hair teenagers with haircuts by vegie-matic, Frankie, the hairy pot belly pig and two old geezers, one dressed as if it's winter, the other with an aluminum beer can glued to his face. The aliens would lay down their lasers and surrender immediately, demanding, no, insisting on safe passage home.

With a little luck, the hairy porker doesn't come over. Dinky told me what a swell guy he is. I rolled my eyes and look out at the ocean for solace.

The porpoises are gone now, replaced by white caps. The wind was picking up. It whipped the line around and I have to hold the pole. I decided to reel it in to check the bait and find that it's gone. I put some more bait on and throw it back in.

I had the same feeling for fishing as when I was a kid. Put some bait on the hook and win a prize. Or don't win a prize. What you win, no one knows. That's the fun of ocean fishing.

Dinky starts telling me about his other offspring. She's thirty-three and a nymphomaniac, who has gone through several husbands and countless boyfriends. She even rode with a biker gang once. I have never met her, thank God. She lives up north mostly. I've seen a picture of her. She's her father's daughter. It's rare for him to talk about her. She must be popping out another grandchild or two for him. She has seven or eight, all different ages and races, all from different men, none living with her.

I felt a tug on the line and reeled it up to check the bait. Dinky thinks I'm leaving, so he got up as well. He then realized that I'm only checking the bait and he sat back down.

"You never catch anything off this stupid pier anymore," he said.

I don't say anything to that and he has a bored or depressed look.

"I have to be going," he said. He got up again and looked confused. I tossed the hooked anchovy back in the water and sat back down.

"So long, Dink," I said to hurry him along.

"Wanna beer?" he offers. He knows I won't accept it but I think one day I will accept the beer, just to see what he would do.

"Nah," I said.

He left with a wave, stopping to talk to someone else he knows. He knows everyone in town. Good old Dink.

A lifeguard jeep drove by on their way to the end of the pier. The lifeguards have a tower near the base of the pier, where they have a small telescope perched on a tripod, usually to spy on young girls on the beach. I should know, because I worked as a lifeguard one summer and that's what we did. Some things never change. They also use the public address system on the tower to warn away the surfers from the swimming area and the swimmers away from the surfers and both from the pier.

The jeep doubled back now. Two blonde, young Adonises sit like Gods in the yellow jeep. They wear dark glasses that reveal very little emotion. One waved at me and grinned, while the other looked away as if he saw something he doesn't like. They drove by and I'm left with the sea, which is okay with me.

The sun is setting now and the pier walkers are young men or middle-age couples in evening clothes, waiting for tables at the restaurant, built at the base of the pier many years ago.

It's getting cooler now. That's the thing about living at the beach. The moist air that blows on shore is so damn cold. Sometimes it blows the other way and we have the Santa Ana winds, a warm, dry wind from the desert.

I don't like the Santa Ana's either, because it makes me feel like a dried up raisin. The surfers love it because the wind hollows the waves out for better surfing. The firefighters hate it because of the brush fires it sometimes starts in the hills behind the city. I hate it because whenever I walk across my carpet, I get a shock, if I touch anything metal. I'm always afraid the shock would stop my heart for good. The Santa Ana's are a hot, dry wind that cracks my lips and plugs up my nose. Everyone thinks that I should move to one of those desert retirement communities in Arizona. Too damn hot for me. I would rather bundle up against the cool, humid, salty air.

A well-dressed middle-age couple walked by. They are not close and from their expressions, it looks as if they have been arguing.

"Damn you," the woman whispers.

"You little slut," the man said a little louder. They are walking away, but I can still hear them.

"Serves you right, you bastard." It was the last thing I heard from the two lovebirds.

I smiled at them. He seemed to be trying to catch up to her. They go to the end of the pier and stopped. I decided when they come back, that I will go to the end of the pier. I reeled up my line and gathered my stuff and when they walk back in stone cold silence, I made my move.

I threw my line back in and sat down to wait. I looked into the cooler and see that I have one more soda left. I already ate the sandwich, but I'm still hungry. I think about eating at the restaurant, but decided against it. I hate to eat at restaurants by myself. Besides this one is too expensive. I will go home and make another sandwich. The thought doesn't appeal to me.

A young couple walked by followed by a couple of kids on skateboards. It is growing darker and the light posts that alternate on each side of the pier, are not turned on yet. The sun is setting fast now, creating a firestorm of reds and oranges on the watery horizon. To the east, comes the invading darkness covering everything like an ominous blanket.

The lights of the city blinked on slowly. It is a plain looking town during the day, but like all cities, it is pretty at night. Like glittering jewels that lay scattered over the hills. It is getting colder, but I don't feel it for some reason. In fact, it seemed to me to be getting warmer.

I reeled in my line and put away my fishing tackle. I stood up, unsure of what to do. The skateboarders raced by me back toward shore, but the young couple was still at the end. They embraced.

I waited in the darkness for a moment looking over the railing at the jet-black water. The couple still does not leave and I think about going, but something held me to the railing.

About the time I turned thirty, I met Lisa. No woman before or since struck me like she did. Why it didn't work I will never know. Sometimes I think it was something I did or didn't do or something I said or didn't say. I always wonder what she is doing now. She's the only woman I can honestly say, that I fell in love with. Sometimes I pretend that we got married and had some kids.

She was in my dreams a lot lately. She spoke to me in them, calling for me to join her. I forget that she never called me when we knew each other, so why would she call me now? I think of her now. She seems everywhere. She is in the inky water as it laps against the pilings. She is in the soft Pacific breeze that blows across the water, swirling around and through everything. She is in the sea odor, the briny aroma of decaying kelp. She is taunting me and I am weakening.

I peered over the railing and saw her face. She has not changed over the years. Her soft face, her deep blue eyes, her soft, silky blonde hair that curled and swirled with delight down to her fine soft shoulders. She's the most beautiful woman I have ever seen, then and now.

I used to compare her to the few other women I dated afterward, but there was no contest. It wasn't just her beauty that I fell deeply in love with. She had a great laugh. Her sense of humor made it hard to believe that she ever got mad or sad. She was also very intelligent, but she did not flaunt it. She was one of those classy people, who came along only once in one's lifetime. I used to daydream about her for hours. I still do. I know it's wrong to do, but I can't help it. I saw her face in the sea now.

I turned around and the young couple has disappeared. I'm not unhappy about that. I'm alone at the end of the pier. The lights of the city twinkle before me like a thousand knowing winks.

A mysterious young woman sauntered toward me from the twinkling lights of the city as if in a dream. She walked slowly and soon her destination is clear. At first I can't make her out because of the darkness. When she got closer, she looks remarkably like Lisa. She hasn't aged a day. She is twenty-five and I'm thirty again. We looked deep into each other's eyes, but I can't read her thoughts. For a few moments we do not speak.

"Lisa?" I whispered.

"Hey."

She humored me with that patent smile of hers. She tossed her head to the side and lowered her eyes like she used to do. My knees almost buckled when she does this.

"Lisa? You're not Lisa?" I asked.

She shook her blonde hair and we stared at each other for a moment. I felt young and foolish again and glad that she was with me.

I blink and she moved past me. I looked around and saw her glide away from me before she disappeared as if into the mist and I returned to the present. I leaned on the railing for support. It's the same railing that I fished from as a kid.

The damp wind blows stronger. I shivered from the cold and my knees still hurt. I accidentally banged my knee on the wooden railing and now it really hurts. I put my hand to my knee to stop the pain. I looked up and the woman disappeared into the night.

I turned back to the water and studied the inviting blackness. My hands are wet from the moisture. They're also white from fear and cold. I looked around and I'm alone on the pier. Just the endless ocean and me.

I gave a sigh that seemed to last a lifetime as I look down into the black water. The water was about twenty feet down. I awkwardly swung my sore skinny leg over the railing and straddled the railing like a horse. I cannot go back to my apartment. Without regret, I followed Lisa into the past of my youth and toward everything that made me happy and whole.

The End

GHOSTLY ILLUISIONS

The girl watched as the lizard suddenly darted out from beneath the rock. The reptile stopped and, using its primitive instincts, surveyed the strange surroundings. It did not see the large animal behind it.

The girl approached carefully, moving into position before making her move, then pounced on the doom lizard. She cupped the reptile in her small hand, feeling the sensation of the small body wiggling for freedom. She rose and ran in the direction of an abandoned barn that stood at the edge of a clearing of trees.

A narrow dirt road, deeply rutted from past rains and worn from travel, ran through the meadow passing the building before veering off into the woods.

The girl skipped lazily through the tall grass, delighted in the sensation of the grass against her bare legs. She stopped in front of the barn door unsure of the darkness inside.

An eerie silence greeted her as she entered the room. When her eyes adjusted she could make out several objects in the room.

She placed the lizard gently in a jar that sat on a table, wrapping a piece of leather over the top and securing it with a piece of string that she fished out of her dress pocket.

She made sure there were holes in the leather for the animal to breathe. She found some matches and lit a storm lantern that sat in the corner.

The flame illuminated the room, slowly revealing an old wooden chair and the wobbly table. The girl felt the excitement grow as the silence and darkness engulfed her. It was an ear splitting ominous stillness.

A foreign noise startled her from her trance and she spun around to find him standing there in the doorway. Anger flushed her face for a brief moment. She spat anger at his intrusion into her semi-dark private world. He stared at her in silence as she rolled her eyes.

"Where have you been?" she snapped.

He shrugged and grinned like an idiot. A wide grin threatened to separate his face. He scratched his head with a large meaty hand and leaned against the door with menacing hunger.

The girl showed no sign of fear in her eyes, only the calm knowledge of confidence. She wore an eerie confidence that went beyond her expression to her very soul.

The man, in his early twenties, was big and broad in size but small and weak in mind. He smiled shyly and played with his wheat color hair that someone, he didn't remember who, had cut very short and somewhat awkwardly. He turned and left the barn without a word or looking back, the grin still planted on his face.

The girl watched from the darkness of the room as he strolled child-like through the meadow, back the way he came. She turned and focused her attention on the stairway that led upstairs. Something seemed to draw her to the stairs that creaked when she stepped on the first rung.

Some of the steps were broken or missing and she slowly and carefully made her way up, holding onto the wooden railing. The landing opened up to a dark room, empty, as was an adjoining room, partitioned off long ago.

The girl could see an angle of the second room due to the missing door. A small object scurried across the floor, followed by another. She had once been afraid of the dark and things that scurried along the floor but she was not afraid anymore.

****

The old man spat on the wooden porch when the youth lumbered up the steps to the store.

"Where the fuck have you been?" the old man asked.

The youth only shrugged at the question, nodding in the direction that he had come.

"You've been at that old place again haven't you?" the old man
said gruffly. "I thought I told you to stay away from there. Bad
things happened there."

He rubbed his gray mustache with the back of his gnarled hand.

"Git inside and sweep up the mess in the aisle," he mumbled.
"Some stupid tourass knocked over another jar of tomato sauce.
Why is it always tomato sauce?"

"I saw her," the idiot youth said with a grin.

"Who?"

"Her," the youth said.

He pointed in the same direction as before.

The old man studied him for a moment then shook his head in
confusion and went back inside his store.

****

It was dark and there was no moon, yet the girl moved unerring
through the backyards, past the barking dogs that sensed
something, but could not see what they were barking at.

She went past dark silent houses, curtains drawn, shades pulled.
The crickets stopped their chorus until she passed, then started up
again when she was gone. She climbed a wooden fence and stalked
past Mr. Johnson's chicken coop.

A cat pawed at the hinged door of the coop trying to get in. It
arched its back up and hissed in alarm as she neared.

She stopped and stared at the cat as if in some lost and forgotten
thought.

The cat hissed again but she ignored it. She brushed a wisp of her
hair from her eyes and continued on, certain of her destination. She
crossed an open field, then an empty street. It was dark despite a
string of electric lights voted in by a recent bond issue.

She crossed the now darken playground of Meadowland
Elementary School. The echoes of unseen children playing in the
playground still haunted her soul. It was well past midnight as she
entered one of the darken classrooms. It was Miss Brady's class.

The girl could almost see the shy spinster with the funny glasses
poised at the blackboard with her book open in one hand and a
piece of white chalk in the other.

She saw the other children squirming in their seats, watching the
clock on the wall above the chalkboard. Freddie and Jack were in

18

the back talking boldly to each other. Susan sat in the front tossing her curly blonde hair around in growing confidence.

The girl opened her eyes and wiped away the tear that formed in the corner of her eye. She studied the silent room lit only by the streetlight, visible through the Venetian blinds. She knew they had recently installed the lights because someone was vandalizing the school.

She knew it was Freddie and Jack since she saw them do it one night. The girl began to sob quietly. After a moment of composure, she went over to her desk and sat down, fingering her name that she carved in the wood several months ago.

She got up and left Miss Brady's sixth grade class, walking slowly down the quiet hallway adorned with a gallery of simple but promising pictures.

She was now out in the playground. She walked over to the swings and sat down, swinging back and forth, dragging one foot across the soil. The chain creaked with protest as the girl increased the arc of her swing. Higher and higher she swung, back and forth, her hair trailing freely behind her. Suddenly she slowed herself down by dragging her feet. She hopped off and wandered the playground not knowing where she was going. She had plenty of time to wander with no real place to go.

****

The woman switched the light on and entered the room. She put a hand to her head as if she forgot something, and then left the room only to come back with a book tucked under her arm and a cup of steaming coffee. She placed the cup down and sat comfortably in the recliner, opening the book in the middle and shuffling the pages to the one she wanted.

Suddenly she dropped the book, almost knocking over the cup and ran into the kitchen. A pan of soup was bubbling over onto the stove.

"Oh dear," she moaned.

When she was through cleaning, she scanned the room as if daring it to create another problem. Satisfied, she went back to the living room where she found the book on the floor. She glanced at the photograph of a young girl, smiling, squinting into the noon sun, her hair ruffled by the March winds.

The sudden ringing caused her to spill the coffee that she balanced on her lap. She looked at the phone as it went silent between rings. It rang again then silence. On the third ring she picked it up, not saying anything.

"Hello, Debbie?" the female voice said. "Debbie. It's Teri."

"Oh. Hi Ter." the woman said. "I thought it was one of those calls again."

"Are you still getting those," the caller said.

"Almost every day," the woman said. "It rang last night but I didn't get to it. It wasn't you was it?"

"No. Maybe you should get an unlisted number," the caller said.

"No. I can't do that."

"Want me to come over?" the caller asked.

Debbie thought she heard music in the background as well as a male voice.

"No. I'm fine. I'm in the middle of a good book," she said.

"Sure you're okay?" her friend asked. "It's not good for you to be alone so much."

"I'm fine," the woman said. "You're sweet to ask."

There was a long pause, which grew uncomfortable after each second.

"Well okay. You know my number. Don't hesitate to call."

"I won't. Bye," the woman said.

Hanging up, she felt even lonelier and wished she talked longer. Maybe she would leave town or take a trip. Deep down she knew she could not leave. The little girl in the picture smiled at her as if she knew her devotion.

The phone calls started just recently. No one spoke, only a soft crackle of static, then silence. As if on cue, the phone rang, startling the woman.

She picked it up hoping it was Teri. Her heart sank and the fear knotted her stomach, as the soft crackle of static seemed to grate her spine and pierce her brain. Suddenly the static vanished, leaving only an eerie silence that seemed to have no boundary.

"Patty," the woman screamed into the phone, then dropped it onto the floor as if it was evil. She held her head as if it was going to explode, trying to grasp reality.

The receiver swung back and forth by its cord, the dial tone now constant. Slowly the woman put the phone back on the cradle staring at it in terror. Minutes passed and it did not ring. The knot of dread grew within her. Dread that it would not ring again and fear that it would.

****

The lumbering giant leaned against the door jam. Foot traffic passed him as if he wasn't there. The old man came out of the store with determination written on his face.

"Hey you," he barked. "Have you cleaned up the back room yet?"

The old man's attention focused on something down the street then it returned to the younger man.

"Yuppp," the young man said.

"Then what the hell are you standing around here for?" the old man snapped. "Go find something to do. I'm sure Mr. Cooper will have something for you to do."

The old man was small in stature as he poised in front of the man-child trying to wear down the younger man with his aged wise glare.

"Sure," the youth said.

With his ever-present grin, he strolled down the street, whistling happily to himself. He saw someone wave to him but he did not respond. He crossed the street unaware of the approaching car that had to slam on its brakes. An angry horn sounding its message. The youth made his way along the sidewalk, his mind elsewhere.

He visualized people coming up to him, asking for advice, begging for his attention and affection. He did not travel in reality, choosing to stay in his own world of illusions. His instincts guiding his physical being somehow while his consciousness played in the field of illusions.

He saw her standing by the lamppost at the intersection. The sun was shining on her flaxen hair creating a halo-like effect. She wore a long paisley dress and she was barefoot. She watched him with cold eyes filled with disdain.

"I did what you ask," he said.

"Did anybody see you?" she asked.

She was not unconvinced even though he shook his head.

"Can I touch your hair?" he asked.

He suddenly reached his large meaty hand out toward her.

She backed away sharply, her eye's narrowing. A serious cloud crossed his face briefly but his sunny disposition returned almost as immediately. She turned to leave but his voice stopped her.

"What's wrong?" he asked.

"Nothing," she said.

He watched her disappear when the shrill voice startled him.

"Artie," a bird-like voice cawed.

He turned toward it with a lazy smile.

"Yessum," he said. He glanced at the woman's face, before politely looking down. He also folded his arms across his chest.

"I have something for you to do. Are you through with your other chores?" the woman asked.

She also folded her arms as if challenging him to an arm folding contest. She tied her iron-streaked hair in her usual tight bun. He had seen her once with her hair down and he almost didn't recognize her.

"Yessum."

"Then come along," she said. Her voice sounded like the snap of a twig on a cold winter day. "Just don't stand there like a buffoon. All the sacks of fertilizers have to be taken from the back room and stacked, neatly, up front near the empty flowerpots. Can you do that?"

"Yessum," he blurted out. He shuffled off in the direction of the back room of the nursery.

"Neatly," she said. She looked around wondering whom he was talking to earlier, but saw no one. She worried about this simple boy but he seemed harmless enough.

****

The woman knelt before the altar, silent for a few moments before she rose and seated herself in the first row of pews. She did not hear the other person slip into the pew behind her. She sensed their presence, turned and smiled at her friend.

"Hi," she whispered.

The other woman smiled warmly putting her arm on her friend's shoulder.

"It hurts so badly," Debbie said.

She saw but did not really see the pew's finely polished wood.

"Why don't we take a trip somewhere," her friend said.

"What about work?" Debbie asked.

"I have some time built up. It'll be fun. We can drive up the

Oregon coast. Or go to the mountains."

"What if she needs me?" Debbie asked.

"Oh, Deb. She's gone. You have to see that."

"I can't. Teri. I see her in everything. I can't pass her room without breaking down. Or when her favorite TV show comes on. Then those phone calls. I know it's her. I don't know what to do. There's no way I can go by the grave. I even drive out of the way to avoid her school. I can't stop. I just..." She started sobbing burying her head in her friend's arms.

"Oh Deb," her friend whispered.

****

The auditorium was full of restless, impatient children sectioned off by grades. Several teachers stood milling around on stage while others sat in a single row of chairs facing the elementary school age students.

A small nervous man, balding but not old, walked onto the stage. His wire frame glasses gleamed brightly from the glare of the florescent lights. The teachers, who were standing, returned to their seats, waiting while the little man stood in front of the microphone. He scanned the auditorium as if looking for someone.

"More than a month..."

The mechanical shrill of the microphone pierced the room and there was a splatter of laughter.

"Can I have your attention? Thank you," he demanded. His attention was focused on the front row.

"More than a month ago, we lost one of our students in a tragic accident, as you are aware. Patricia Walker was one of our brightest and best loved students and I can speak for all of us when I say we miss her dearly."

He stopped and wiped his forehead with a handkerchief, then adjusted his glasses. He did not see several of the teachers behind him wiping their eyes. The children shifted nervously in their seats.

"I just have a few announcements. First there have been rumors in the press and elsewhere that her death was not an accident. I want to make it perfectly clear that according to our fine police department, there is still no evidence of this rumor and as far as I am concern, this was just a tragic accident. Next there have been a several incidents of vandalism in our classrooms. The police think it is being done at night despite the city's recent addition of streetlights. I assure you that whoever is doing this will be caught and severely punished."

The principal stopped to let the threat sink in. He scanned the room settling on two of the students he knew were the culprits but could not prove yet. The boys shifted uncomfortably in their seats, staring at their knees.

"I want to thank everyone for the donations for the nice tombstone," he said. "Mrs. Walker also wants to thank everyone for their letters and cards. There is even talk about renaming the school after Patricia."

A spattering of applause broke out.

"Next month is an annual spelling bee between the grades," he said dabbing at his forehead again. "Two students from each class will be picked. I urge you to volunteer for the bee."

"The winners will get prizes and participation will be counted as extra credit," he said. "Also next month is 'Parents Night' Please urge your parents to attend. There will be refreshments. It will helpful for the teachers to meet your parents. Memo's for the spelling bee and Parents Night will be passed around in the next day or so."

He looked back at the teachers behind him but they stared blankly back at him as he adjusted his glasses.

"Are there any questions?" he asked.

He knew there wouldn't be anyway and when no one raised their hands, he turned back to the teachers behind him.

"If there are no comments from the staff..." He paused then went on. "Then everyone is excused... in an orderly manner. Thank you," he said.

Smiling weakly, he turned back to the teachers aware of the departing students behind him but unaware of the large young man who watched the assembly from the back of the room. The young man leaned on a broom as he watched the children leave from the three exits.

If the little bald man could stand in front of everyone, then why couldn't he, he thought? He could have the same control. They would all be listening to him with the same intent. The tough looking six-graders would look at him in awe, while the girls would flirt with him and vie for his attention. He saw himself being asked questions. Even the funny bald man with his few remaining strands of hair combed down over the baldness, would want his opinion on some important matter.

"Are you supposed to be doing something?" the voice said. The voice seemed to filter its way through the dissipating fog.

The balding principal stood in front of him with his black eyes narrowing. The young man frowned to counteract the silliness of the bald man.

"Young man, if you're supposed to be working I suggest you do it," the principal snapped.

The youth steeped back as if slapped, gripping the broom handle tightly. He lumbered off without looking back.

"That Jackson boy sure is a weird one," the woman said from behind the principal.

The principal turned and forced a practiced smile.

"Just a little slow is all."

"He gives me the creeps," the woman said. "I don't know why he was hired with all these children around."

"His mother says that he's harmless," the principal said.

The woman teacher snorted and shaking her head with a shudder and slowly walked away. The nervous bald man wiped his forehead again and walked back to his office.

****

The young man watched the children outside, leaning against his broom. He watched as a sixth grader slid down a slide exposing a bare thigh. He smiled at that and felt the inflated stirring. He turned and saw the figure by the lunch tables and the feeling left.

She did not appear to see him as she scanned the other children at play in the schoolyard. She had a look of hurt and envy mixed into the chalky whiteness of her face. She saw him and rolled her eyes in mock disgust, but he didn't understand the gesture.

"I guess that I'm famous," she said.

"Not as famous as me," he said.

"As I," she corrected.

She gave him that look that all eleven-year-olds have, especially when they know that they are right.

"As me," he defended.

"Jeese Louise. You're stupid," she said.

She had a hard time believing that someone older than her was so much slower. It delighted her in knowing that.

He sat down next to her at the table, too close to her liking. She rose and pointed a finger at him. She did not know why she hated him so much. Was it because he was an adult or that he was a man, she did not know?

"If you so much as tell a soul, so help me God."

"I won't," the young man whined. "I promise."

"You better not," she said coldly. "And if you go near her..."

"I won't," he repeated shaking his head. "I won't. I said I won't."

She turned sharply and walked away, heading toward a group of other children who clustered in small clichés. A few were off by themselves, staring at the ground in shyness.

Occasionally they would glance around. They would probably grow up rich and famous, she thought. She had always detested the quiet, shy ones. They were usually fat or unattractive, always different from everyone else. She had always been the instigator in teasing them, the geeks, the nerds.

She went up to Paul Farnsworth. He was a thin bespectacled boy with thin dark hair and a pale almost feminine face. He stood alone next to a wall. He did not look up when she approached him nor did he notice when she laughed in his face.

She laughed at his ugliness, his awkwardness. The boy shuddered as if he was suddenly very cold.

A loud buzzer went off and he shuffled off to class followed by the other students. Some ran while others chased their friends.

None seemed to notice the girl as they passed her on all sides. It was good that they did not see her for they would have seen the tears on her face.

She had been the most popular girl in school. Boys, whom she detested yet scared her, were now reacting differently to her lately, before the accident. She knew that it was no accident. She knew who caused the fall, knew who planned for her to be in the barn by the meadow, and who knew that she always played there. She knew who it was and he would pay. They would all pay in time, the fat and the ugly and the shy and the miserable.

****

The woman fumbled with the flowerpot, spilling some of the dark earth. She finally succeeded in getting the plant out and into the small hole she had dug. She did not see the man as he approached. She sensed his presence and turned and gasped at his presence.

"Oh. What do you... Who are you?" she mumbled.

He stood in silence with a grin and his fists jammed in his pockets and spoke after a few moments.

"Are you Mrs. Walker?" he asked.

"Yes. What do you want?" she asked. "Who are you?"

"I work at the school sometimes," he said. "The school where she went."

"Ohhhh. What do you want?" the woman said.

She felt her legs go numb and her heart freeze.

"I saw her at school," the young man said.

"Who, by the grace of God are you?" the woman asked.

"Patty. I saw her at school," he said.

He was not prepared for the woman's reaction.

"Get the hell out of here before I call the cops," she screamed. She held a small weed-eater clutched tightly in her fist, raising it as if ready to strike. He stepped back in defense, confused.

"I thought you would be happy. I saw her. I talked to..."

The woman threw the weed-eater at him hitting him in the chest. He backpedaled in shock and pain. He was sure that she would be happy. His small mind could not comprehend the woman's actions. He did not feel the pain; instead he was shocked by the trickle of blood.

"Get the hell out of my yard," she screamed.

"But I...." he stuttered.

Retreating from the garden, he found himself in front of the plain one-story house bordered on both sides by other plain single-story homes. He started to run, when he saw the woman run into the house, the screen door slamming in condemnation.

A small crowd of neighbors came outside and watched the large youth run away. They talked among themselves, shaking their heads and pointing.

The girl sat across the street, her legs crossed, and her blonde hair behind her. Her face was a cauldron of emotions, and her eyes aflame with anger and revenge. Her emotions suddenly shifted when the woman came back out of the house with a baseball bat. The girl recognized it as her own softball bat.

"Momma," the girl cried. She spoke so softly that the woman

across the street did not hear. The girl got up slowly and walked toward her mother. "Momma," she cried. Her face was wet with tears. "Momma. Jesus God. Momma," she screamed hysterically.

The woman sensed something and looked around. It was as if someone was calling her, but she heard only the wind and saw only the summer breeze.

"Oh my God," the woman said, falling to her knees.

"Debbie. What's wrong?" a neighbor said. She put a hand on Debbie's shoulder. The contact seemed to set off an alarm.

"She's here. I can feel her," the woman sobbed.

"Who?"

"She's here. Dear God. I know she's here," Debbie sobbed. She allowed herself to be guided back to the house.

The screen door slammed hard which startled the girl back to reality. She stood alone among the newly planted garden, and then slumped to the ground. Pain etched on her face and her soundless wail going unheard except for the large tomcat whose instinct warned it of danger.

****

The oafish young man fumbled with his keys, finally unlocking the stubborn door. He entered the Spartan apartment feeling secure in the darken room. He relocked the dead bolt, paused as if trying to hear something then went over to a stale mattress that lay on the floor in the corner.

He was immune to the odor that penetrated the mustiness and dankness. The only other room in the apartment was a small cramped bathroom that smelled worse. The cracked mirror reflected back several different images of his large ruddy face. He took his shirt off and examined his chest. He splashed cold water on himself and watched the red tinted water drained into the soiled basin. The pain subsided and he tried to calm himself.

He did not see the cockroach that scurried across the floor. The hysterical woman had confused him. He was puzzled by her actions. Wouldn't she be glad that he had talked to her daughter? Wouldn't that mean she wasn't dead? If she could talk and be seen? They did bury her several weeks ago, when he had to dress up nicely. He wore that suit with the tie that strangled his throat.

He remembered the girl's mother and the hysterical scene she made. He felt important as he viewed the small body lying in the simple but tasteful casket. He smiled when she opened her eyes and stared at him and him alone and flung daggers of accusations at him. She looked so pretty, despite the purplish bruises on her neck.

He stared at the ceiling. A discoloration formed in the corner where the moisture of past rains had condensed. His thoughts were not on the stains but of the crowd before him. He spoke to them in his mind, seeing their attentive gazes. They, in turn laughed at his jokes, cheered his accomplishments and applauded his ambitions. He smiled at the ceiling in triumph.

A sudden rap on the window startled him out of his illusions. As he pulled up the shade, the glass shattered in a thousand pieces. He covered his face in defense, but it was too late. He felt the sting of glass piercing his face and arms, like stinging ants.

Blinking his eyes to make certain that he could still see, he uncovered his arms and touched his face. He saw the blood on his fingers and felt the rise of panic. He rushed to the mirror and what he saw caused him to gasp. He splashed water on his face, the coolness calmed him somewhat. The ugly rips on his pale face shocked him.

"Omigod. Omigod," he repeated. "Omi-gosh. Sweet Jesus help me."

He left the bathroom fumbling with the lock and stumbled down the stairs out into the street. He wasn't sure where he was headed.

Several people stared at him, some pointing rudely at him. The youth ignored them and ran to the grocery store for help. Several customers waited impatiently in line at the counter, clutching their items as if expecting someone to steal them.

The old man looked up from the cash register as he handed a woman's change back to her. At first there was anger, but then he saw the fear in the youth's face.

"What the hell happened to you?" he said. "You look like you got the shit beaten out of you. Oh, pardon me Mrs. Stewart."

"The window just shattered," the youth whined.

The old man rubbed his fingers on his grizzled chin and inspected the damage.

"Go down to Doc Harwood's clinic and he'll fix you up," the old man said. "Now. Go away. I'm busy."

The youth waited as if there was something more for him to say then turned and sauntered out of the store making his way to the doctor's office several blocks away.

****

The girl watched as the youth lumbered up the stairs to his apartment. She could see the stitches and bandages on his face. She smiled warmly as he let himself into his apartment.

He closed the door but it didn't matter since she was already inside. She watched him as he examined himself in the mirror. For a brief moment, she actually felt sorry for him when she detected fear and vulnerability on his face. The pity quickly turned back to hatred and the lights suddenly went off.

He started to panic, unable to see. He bumped hard into the wall before he fumbled on the floor. He crawled to his mattress feeling secure. Nothing could happen there as he cradled his pillow. He laid down feeling the effects of the Novocain. He felt the room spin and closed his eyes to stop the pain. When he reopened them he saw her standing over him, her hands on her hips. He held the pillow in front of him in terror.

"What do you want?" he asked.

He wished she would simply go away but her icy stare did not change.

"You," she spat.

The youth buried his head in the pillow to block out the illusion.

"No. No," he cried.

The words were lost in the echo of the word 'You'. The echo slowly died away and the only sound was his own. Sobbing, he peeked from the pillow to discover that he was alone.

****

The woman studied herself in the mirror. She seemed to have aged twenty years in the past month. Dark shadows were visible beneath her eyes. She tossed her short auburn hair, and then made a face at herself, forcing herself to smile. She could not and turned away. She splashed water on her face and groped for a towel.

She looked into the mirror and was about to leave when something caught her eye. She turned, but saw nothing. She pushed opened the bathroom door and looked into her bedroom but saw

30

nothing. Out of habit she glanced at the phone, and then quickly left the room.

She didn't stop as she passed the closed door to the girl's room, until she was in the neat but small living room. She glanced back down the hallway and started for the kitchen when a noise stopped her. She froze and her heart sank as she waited in the silence. She stole a glance at the door down the hallway, as the noise continued.

It was like someone was dragging something heavy across gravel. It got louder and louder as the woman back pedaled with fear. The noise suddenly stopped and the door to the girl's room opened slowly, scraping across the carpet. The woman felt herself being drawn down the hallway. She tried to resist, but could not.

She could see an angle of the room, a corner of the small bed and part of the dresser. She stood in the doorway for the first time in over a month. Everything was as it was before, the dresser with a variety of toys and stuffed animals on it.

A large poster of the latest boy band covered one wall to the right of the dresser. A small desk and chair sat in the corner beneath the poster. A lamp sat on the desk, a doll figurine topped by a dull yellow shade. The figurine, its rosy cheeks and painted smile seemed to study the woman. The narrow bed with a pink quilt on it sat beside a dresser covered with more stuffed animals of various sizes and shapes and colors. A night table sat on the other side of the bed with a digital clock on it. Various pictures and posters dotted the wall but the woman's attention focused on the stuffed animals, their glassy eyes focused on her. A tiger growled at her with cotton fangs and a Koala bear in a climbing position seemed to ignore her.

She glanced at the closet door across the room. Slowly she drew closer, daring herself to open the French doors. Just as she was about to reach for the handles, the doors flew open.

She jumped back in shock to cover the scream that never came. A small toy-like rocking chair lay on the floor of the closet. The woman let a muted moan when she saw the bloodstain sweatshirt that was draped over the chair. Across the front of the black sweat shirt with red letters were the words Trail Blazers.

****

The little girl watched him approach from the upstairs window.

31

He seemed out of place among the multi-colored flowers that dotted the meadow. She noticed a slight limp hampered his walk.

His attention solely focused on the two-story structure that stood in the clearing at the edge of the pine forest. The young man ambled along the dirt road and when he got to the doorway of the house, he stopped. He glanced back at the swaying grass of the meadow before he went into the darkness. It took a moment for his eyes to adjust and when they did he saw that he was alone.

The only furniture was a small table in the middle of the room. A lone unlit candle sat on the table. In the corner, dark and foreboding was the staircase that led upstairs.

He made his way to the foot of the stairs when a flicker of light upstairs caught his attention. He started up the stairs slowly, feeling the instinctive urge to shift his weight when going up the stairs.

Suddenly one of the rungs, rickety with age, gave way and his leg crashed through the stairs to his knees. He caught himself with his hands on the rise above. Realizing that he was okay, he pulled himself up and continued on.

The room before him became more visible as he ascended. The room was small and completely bare. A heavy black drape hung over the single window shutting out most of the light. He looked into the second room. The doorless opening exposed a small angle. When he entered the second room, his instincts told him that he was not alone.

A small black shape scurried across the floor. Where he felt secure in the darkness of his own apartment, he felt afraid and vulnerable in this room. A noise behind him made him jump. It wasn't a sound that had a beginning or an end. It was a noise that always seemed to be there. A scraping ominous sound. He did not know why he failed to hear it before. The lone window was also covered with a heavy drape, hanging down in gloom.

In the corner of the room was a rocking chair, suddenly there, as if for the first time. It rocked back and forth. At first it was hardly noticeable but when he looked at it, it rocked faster and faster.

Suddenly it stopped and she approached, her blank eyes penetrating his soul. She did not say anything, only turned and with a half-smile drew back the drapes. The onslaught of sunshine blinded him momentarily. He failed to notice that the glass was missing. It appeared to have been recently broken. She looked at him with full fury and she pointed to the window. He shook his head and sweat formed on his pale face.

"I.. I.. thought we were friends," he said. He found himself drawn slowly toward the window.

"You're all alike," the girl seethed. "You're weak and stupid and clumsy." She pointed a small accusing finger at him. "You don't deserve to live. I hate you. I hate you all."

He trembled at the voice, but he could not move or turn away.

She pointed to the window and again he shook his head in fear. He found himself moving closer and closer to the window, unable to stop himself. He tried to grab a corner but a sharp pain rocketed through him as the shard of broken glass pierced his hand. He watched the blood poured freely from the wound.

She watched with glee as he fell to the ground below. He had broken his neck in the fall; his head twisted grotesquely back up toward her. His eyes were open in shock. His mouth, blood trickling from the side, formed into a smile.

The girl felt nothing anymore. No relief or remorse, nor hatred or pity. She turned from the window and sat down in the rocking chair, rocking back and forth. The gentle warm summer breeze played with her hair and she waited patiently knowing that he would return to haunt her for ever and ever.

The End

WALK IN THE DESERT

The stifling hot, dry air sucked the strength from his soul. The heat from the hard ground seemed to seep through his tennis shoes with the onslaught of the rising morning sun.

The small, foreign pickup truck rolled to stop with its engine off. A young man, tired from the drive yet excited by the adventure, got out and scanned the dusty parking lot. Parked nearby were two passenger cars and an old black van.

Mark adjusted his daypack, heavy with two bottles of water and shifted the 35mm camera on his shoulder. He noticed the sign at the start of the trail.

Two arrows pointed to the east, one denoting a short hike to a peak in the distance, looping back to the desert campgrounds.

The other pointed to an unseen destination, Lost Palm Oasis. The six-mile trail snaked its way up a ravine, then up and over a rise before disappearing.

There was a small metal box with a coin slot next to the sign. Opening the lid, he found various brochures on desert life published by the National Park Service. He took one of each while putting a dime in the slot.

He started out on the wide easy trail. He was surprised at the amount of vegetation as well as the colors. From a distance, the land looked so barren, but up close there were a variety of animal and plant life. Mojave yucca and Creosote bush dominated the small valley. Rodents, reptiles, coyotes and small birds found whatever shade they could from the sun. He reached the rise and turned back to see his small truck in the distance.

The terrain flattened out into gentle rolling hills and small dry washes. Large cliffs rose abruptly to the left as he walked. As heat began to take its toll, he adjusted his daypack, fingering the lens of the camera without thinking.

After a while, he stopped and scanned the scenery, reveling in the solitude and the eerie quiet. Only the lone chirping from a nearby locust broke the dry silence. A gentle breeze from the west played like a ghost on his consciousness.

The trail rose sharply up a steep incline and at the top were two signs. The one facing him had the name and mileage of his destination, while the other faced in the opposite direction with the mileage back to the parking lot. A side trail zigzagged toward an opening in the cliffs to the left. He felt hot and thirsty but decided against taking a drink until later.

He took the camera and focused it on the surrounding vista and then on the cliffs. He shot off several frames of the unusual reddish brown rock formations and creepy dark crevices in the cliff.

He stopped again and drank from the plastic water bottle. Suddenly he heard a noise ahead of him. Two men who looked to be in their 30s walked into view.

For a second sheer panic, then annoyance set in, annoyance at the intrusion into the quiet world and the loss of the fantasy. Both men wore fanny packs and both were sweaty and red-faced as they approached.

The first was tall man with thin, dark hair and a thin beard, who mumbled something as he passed. The other was shorter with light thin hair and wondered out loud how it was going.

"Okay," Mark said with a smile.

They passed and he was back to the increasingly growing solitude. He did not dare to look back until the hikers were out of sight.

The trail made its way across a wide, sandy riverbed before snaking up a dusty ridge. A Palo Verde tree, its branches bright green, sprang out from the middle of the dry bed as if surprising someone.

The terrain leveled off once again but the steep cliffs to the left were no longer in view. Rock formations dotted the landscape here and there, like sentries on duty. He felt the toll of the heavy heated air and took another sip of water.

After a while, the trail wound its way into a deep narrow valley, appearing out of nowhere. Mark guessed the oasis was nearby. He rounded a bend in the trail and stopped suddenly.

The girl looked so unreal yet she was actually standing there. She looked very old, yet she was soft and beautiful with youth. She looked withered and as dead as the surrounding desert, yet she was alive and vibrant as the sparse vegetation.

She stared at him with her pale green eyes. A hidden smile played on her soft pale face despite the sun.

He fidgeted with the camera unsure of what to do. Her presence surprised him, since she had no pack of any kind or any water. She wore a long cotton dress that flowed to her boots, its style and pattern out of place with the rugged environment. She studied him, shocked by his shorts and his t-shirt.

"Who… are you?" he stammered, shielding his eyes from the sun.

"Melinda Douglas," she answered her voice dry as the wind. "What is yours?" she asked, still looking at her shorts.

"Mark," he said. "Mark Stone. Are you from around here?"

"San Francisco. And you?"

"L.A. Riverside actually," he said, but she didn't seem to hear. "Are you by yourself?"

"My father is a gold miner in Mecca," she said. "I haven't seen him in several years. I was on my way there, when my horse ran off."

"Where's Mecca?"

"To the south, I think. They told me to follow this trail."

"I didn't know they allowed horses in the park," he said. Confused, he looked around for her horse.

"What park?" she asked.

"This… Never mind. I guess one can get permission. I'm heading that way, if you want to join me," he offered.

She paused as if to consider the choices. "Thank you," she said glad for the company. "You're so kind."

He didn't carry a gun and she thought that was odd. They walked in silence for a short distance before she noticed the camera.

"What is that?"

"This?" he laughed in surprise but her expression was serious. "It's a camera."

"Haven't you seen a camera before?" he said when she looked

quizzically at him.

"Oh, yes," she said a little hurt. "Just not one like that."

"It's one of those foreign models," he said.

She looked at him in confusion.

"Why don't you wear trousers?" she asked after a moment.

"Cause, it's too hot," he said puzzled.

He studied her odd-looking dress that fell down over black riding boots. The material seemed Spartan, the pattern bland and without color. She turned to face him, her wispy, shoulder-length hair, flowed freely in the dry breeze.

"Are you coming?" she asked her hands seductively on her hips.

He smiled and followed her, feeling happy and at ease by her presence. She had a free spirit about her. They walked in silence before she broke the stillness.

"What do you do for a living?"

"I work for a sporting goods store in Riverside," he said. "But I'm going to school at night."

"Oh," she said confused. "What are you studying?"

"Law," he said. He beamed even though he had taken only one class of pre-law.

"What do you do?" he asked.

"I just returned from school back east."

"Oh yeah? Where?"

"Vassar."

"Where's that?"

"In Virginia," she said.

She stopped suddenly her eyes wide with fear.

"Do you hear that?" she whispered.

She crouched down almost to her knees.

"No, what?" he asked alarmed looking around in confusion. "What are you afraid of?"

"Get down," she hissed. "They'll see you."

"Who?" he spun around, scanning the hills around them.

She didn't answer her eyes still wide with fright. A few awkward moments went by and she rose slowly, the caution ebbing from her.

"What are you on? Some trip or something?" he asked instantly regretting his tone.

She didn't say anything.

"What are you afraid of?" he wondered.

"They're gone. It does not matter."

"Who's they?" he asked.

But she didn't seem to hear him as she walked off.

He stared after her, attracted by her beauty, mystified by her.

The air was still and hot as the sun arced its way down toward the horizon.

"How far is it to this place?"

"Mecca? I don't know. My father said it was a day's ride from Twenty-Nine Palms."

"I'm only going as far as Lost Palm Oasis, which isn't far," he said. "Are you going to stay in Mecca very long?"

She only shrugged her eyes on the rugged cliffs above them.

The trail took a deep descent down into a narrow canyon following a narrow streambed. The canyon walls rose sharply above them, blocking out the sun.

A large Chuckawalla slithered across a rock and disappeared into a dark crevice. Neither human paid any attention to it.

The trail then left the dry bed and made its way up a hill. When they crested the hill they saw a large cluster of palm trees perched in a side canyon.

"That must be Lost Palms oasis," Mark said.

The trail sloped down again crossing a ravine before ascending over another hill. A crudely made sign pointed toward the trees with the word 'oasis' on it. Another sign further up the trail pointed toward a gap between two mountains. The word 'Mecca' was etched in that sign.

"Was this as far as you were going?" she asked looking around.

He just nodded his head.

"Well, I suppose we should part company," she said with a smile. "It was nice meeting you."

"Sure. Maybe I could look you up in Mecca, if that's okay."

"Yes," she said. "That would be all right. Just ask for John Douglas and someone will point out the house to you."

"I'll do that," he said.

He watched her disappear over the next rise.

He suddenly felt very lonely. He started down a series of switchbacks that led down the face of the canyon.

A cluster of palm trees sat in a dry bed at the intersection of the main canyon and a smaller one. The footing was treacherous and several times he caught himself from falling.

He finally found himself at the bottom, not far from the trees. Several small pools of stagnant water sat near the base of the trees. He sat down in the shade and unbuckled his daypack. He drank from the water, then unwrapped a banana and ate it slowly. He decided to save the sandwich and pear for later.

He looked up in time to see her coming toward him. She looked as if she was an apparition emerging mysteriously from the cliffs. She smiled and stood over him.

"I thought you were headed for Mecca?" he said. He shielded his eyes from the sun to see her.

"I lied," she said. "I don't have a father who lives in Mecca. I don't even have a father." She pouted as if a small child.

"I don't understand," he said.

"It doesn't make any difference who I am does it?" she snapped with venom. "The question is who you are?"

Before he could answer she was upon him standing tall over him.

"Why don't you carry a gun? And you don't wear long pants. Don't you fear the hostiles?" She threw the questions at him so fast he almost ducked.

"Who? What hostiles?"

"The Indians of course. The Serranos."

"Indians?" he said. "They're on reservations or in bars or at home. Besides it's illegal to carry guns in the park."

"What's this park you keep talking about?"

"This park. Joshua Tree National Park."

"You mean like Yellowstone Park in Montana?" she said. She struggled to comprehend the strange words she was hearing.

"Something like that, yeah."

"Your clothes and that camera look so strange," she added.

"Thanks," he said. "You're not exactly Cheryl Tiegs in that dress. You look like something from the 1880's."

"This is the 1880's," she breathed, her face ashen.

"Yeah, right," he said, convinced she was crazy. "It's 2004."

"You must be joking," she said. She shook her head and stepped away from him as if he was a monster.

He rose slowly, a creepy feeling seeping through him.

"What year do you think this is?"

"1886. Why don't you..."

"Come off it, lady," he scoffed. "Do you think I fell off the turnip truck yesterday? It's 2004. Time travel only belongs in movies."

Whatever game she was playing, she played it well, he thought.

"We can't be from different times," she said. "It's impossible."

"This is giving me the creeps," he said. "You're not kidding, are you? You actually believe this is the 1880's? Time travel is just TV. It's not real."

She said nothing, her eyes wide with fear.

"It's a great costume and all that. You went to a lot of trouble but..."

He stopped when she glared at him with her fists on her hips. "I don't believe this," he said shaking his head.

"I am from 1886," she said slowly, hiding her growing anger.

"So you think you're from the past. The past is the past and this is the present," he said.

"But you are from the future and this is the present," she countered.

"No way. This is now, 2004. You're from the past. What am I saying? You're not from the past. You're just high on some drugs."

She broke up in laughter. He felt stupid but allowed himself a smile.

"What are you laughing at?"

"Nothing," she said from behind her hand. She giggled some more as Mark sat back down on the boulder.

"You know, you could be the one that's out of place. Or I should say time," she said

"I just left my car back at the parking lot. How do you explain that?" he countered.

"What's a car?" she said.

She smiled as he threw his arms in the air.

"How do you explain this camera? That should prove this is 2004."

She didn't say anything.

"What the hell year is this?" he screamed at the palm trees.

"What difference does it make anyway?"

"It makes a big difference. Because one of us is in the wrong time period, if you're telling the truth. Are you ready for cars and TV's and space shuttles and rock music?"

When she didn't answer, he went on.

"I'm not too anxious to live with gunfighters and Billy the Kid and outlaws. Doesn't sound very safe."

"Billy the Kid was killed several years ago," she said with a smirk. "Besides is it any safer in your era? Don't you have criminals and outlaws anymore? Is it such a perfect time?" Her voice was cold and ominous.

He looked at her and nodded. "Yeah, I guess you have a point."

"I hope society has improved," she said.

"I don't think it's possible that I am in your time," he said.

"Why is that?"

"Because in the 1880's, my parents were not born yet. Neither were my grandparents. So how could you explain my existence?" he asked.

She only shrugged.

"How do you explain my being here?" she retorted after a moment.

"Look. We're here and that's all that matters," he said, tired of the idea. "Do you have a boyfriend?" he asked.

For some reason, he felt relieved when she shook her head.

"How about you?" she asked.

He shook his head and she smiled. There was a silence but it was not awkward.

He focused the camera on her and she acted out several poses. He focused the lens and shot off several frames. She giggled as she made faces at the camera. In jest, she climbed a boulder and stood on top like a mountain climber. Suddenly she lost her balance and he managed to catch her.

"My goodness," she gasped, half laughing.

They looked into each other eyes for a moment before she stood up.

"I'm old enough to be your grandmother," she teased.

"I don't care."

He tried to kiss her but she moved away.

"You're beautiful," he whispered.

"For an old woman. I'm just an old grandmother. Pretty sprite for someone my age. About a hundred and fourteen?" she calculated with a perplexed look.

"Better looking than Za Za Gabor."

"Who?" she asked, a sliver of jealousy crossing her marble color face.

"Just some old actress, who's almost as old as you are."

She felt so good and soft in his arms.

"What if this is my era?" she whispered.

"Then I'll have to adjust," he said. "I'll wear a six shooter and learn to ride a horse."

The girl slid away from him and slowly strolled along the dry bed. He watched her as she turned and smiled back at him.

"Where are you going?" he asked.

She didn't answer and went behind several large boulders. He waited several minutes and she did not return.

"Melinda?" he called out, feeling a rise of panic. "Melinda?"

Suddenly out of nowhere, she reappeared.

"Where..." He stopped and tried to smile. "I thought you left," he said, relieved for some reason.

She scanned the surrounding cliffs, stark brown against the blue sky,

"It's getting late. Another couple of hours and it will be dark," she said. She studied the hues the setting sun made on the cliffs.

"Are you hungry?"

"A little," she admitted.

She watched him pull food from the strange looking pack.

"Thank you," she said taking the sandwich.

"It's turkey on rye," he explained.

"It looks so shiny."

She looked at the sandwich as if it was from another planet.

He laughed and unwrapped it and handed it back to her.

"It's plastic. To keep it fresh," he explained.

She took a bite slowly as if it might be poison.

"I have some fruit too," he offered, tossing an orange to her.

"This, we do have in my time," she said.

After they ate they took drinks from the bottles.

"What are you looking at?" she asked.

"You,"

"We can't stay here you know."

"Why not?" he wondered.

"I don't have a bedroll, nor do we have any blankets."

"I have some back at the car."

"It's getting dark and there is only a partial moon tonight," she said.

"I won't be cold and we can even make a fire," he said.

She didn't reply, noting his lack of concern.

Later that night, as the coals of the fire glowed dimly; they leaned against the boulder in each other's arms, feeling safe and secure. They did not talk. It was not necessary. The stars were bright and stood out against the blackness. It was not cold, but there was a cool crispness to the air.

In the distance, an eerie yip of a coyote echoed through the canyon. Mark felt the girl shudder. A noise in the bushes startled them and Mark strained his senses peering into the darkness.

Mark drifted into a fitful sleep, only to wake with a start. The sky was just beginning to lighten in the east. The shadows of darkness slowly disappear to reveal reality. Dark shapes became Ocotillo plants. Menacing phantoms reformed into palm trees. The air was clean and cool as dawn approached. The peaks of the mountains were catching the first rays of the sun.

She stirred herself awake and looked up at him.

"Morning," he whispered. "How did you sleep?"

"A little stiff, but otherwise all right. And you?"

"Perfect," he said. "Hungry?"

He shifted his position to reach into the pack. He pulled out an apple, which they shared.

"We should head back to the truck," he said.

"I hate for it to end," she said in a strange tone.

"Who says it has to end?" he said.

She sensed his distress and caressed his cheek.

"Let's go," he said after a moment.

They got up and embraced as if to face a coming battle. She felt good in his arms as he held her. They parted and he gathered his pack and the camera.

The trail back passed like a blur to Mark. The heat of the morning was already evident. He took a drink and passed the bottle to the girl but she refused.

"You have to drink something or you will get dehydrated."

"You worry too much," she said.

They walked in silence for a ways.

"Wait till you see my stereo system," he said. "Then again, you've never watched TV or a jet ski or even a radio. Talk about culture shock."

"Your words are so strange."

"Wait till the guys at work see you," he beamed. "The parking lot. You should be able to see it at the top of the rise," he added pointing up the trail. Suddenly he stopped, fearful as he gazed at the rise. "What if there is no parking lot?" he asked, without looking at her.

"Then you would be with me," she said.

What propelled him to start running he didn't know. Maybe fear or panic. He wasn't in good shape and was breathing hard but he didn't slow his pace. As the top of the hill came closer, he could see more and more of the horizon beyond the distant barren hills.

The small truck sat in loyal silence in the lot. Only a small sedan accompanied the truck. With relief, he let out a holler and turned to look for the girl, but she was not there.

"Melinda," he screamed.

He ran back down the trail back to where he left her. He searched everywhere, but he was alone.

"Noooo," he wailed and started back toward the oasis.

He ran helter skelter along the trail, finally falling in exhaustion to the hot earth. He felt dizzy as the bright sun seemed to blur and everything began to spin.

"Are you okay?" The foreign voice seemed friendly.

Mark looked up and saw three Asians standing over him. Two men and a woman dressed in running shorts and T-shirts with various sayings or logos on them. Cameras hung from all three necks. One man helped Mark to his feet.

"Are you okay?" the man repeated.

"No, I mean yeah," Mark fumbled. "Did you see a woman? About so tall. Blonde hair and wearing a funny looking dress?" he asked.

The three Japanese looked at each other in confusion, and shook their heads.

"We came from parking lot and we saw no one else," one man said. "If someone is missing, maybe you should call the authorities?"

The man was short with jet-black hair. Mark started back toward his car, when the voice stopped him.

"Your camera and your pack, sir."

Mark looked at the camera and a wave of awareness overwhelmed him. He grabbed his stuff without thanking the tourists and ran back to his car.

At the top of the rise, he looked back at where he last saw her, but only saw the three tourists making their way along the trail, stopping to take a picture or point at something.

It seemed a lifetime since yesterday. He fumbled for his keys as an eerie feeling engulfed him. He had the notion that he was not alone. The drive into Palm Springs seemed to take forever.

He pulled off the freeway in search of a shopping center. He pulled into a parking lot where there was a one-hour film store. He took the camera and carefully rewound the film wishing he had a digital camera He hurried into the store and handed it to the clerk. She took it without interest.

"Your name?" she asked.

He gave her the information, which she wrote slowly on the package.

"How long will it take?" he asked impatiently.

She looked at him as if was from another planet. "One hour. Duh."

He took the receipt and went outside to wait. In the distance, he thought he saw a young blonde in a green dress, crossing the street.

"Melinda," he yelled after her, but she didn't turn around.

"Melinda," he hollered again, running after her.

She finally turned around but she was not her.

The hour passed slowly and when it was time he went to the counter, where the same bored girl stared back at him.

She asked for the last name, searching the files for the envelope. Mark grabbed them and started to tear it open.

"Hey. That's $4.65 sir," she called out, alarmed.

He pulled out a $5 bill and handed it to her and walked out of the store.

"Sir, your change," she called after him, but he didn't stop.

He tore open the envelope and thumbed through the color prints. What he saw made him drop the photos.

The counter girl looked up as he let out a cry. She watched the man drop some of the pictures and run to his car. She went outside and picked up the pictures. She saw nothing unusual about it. The photos had come out well. The dark blue of the sky contrasted with the several shades of browns of the desert.

The pictures seemed harmless enough. Some were of desert scenes. A few pictures were of a young girl, pretty, but in an old fashion dress. The girl smiled under a bright sun that seemed to illuminate her golden hair.

The End

DESERT HEAT

The road curved to the right and disappeared beyond the car headlights and the canyon wall that rose on each side. The canyon widened out and I could see the vast empty desert in the three quarter moonlight.

Darken mountains rose in the distance while Saguaro cactus stood like unshaven men on sentry duty. The road followed a dry bed for several miles then snaked up a small rise, before dropping down along another dry arroyo.

Something darted off the left. Whatever it was, it was small and quick. I checked the gas gauge again, knowing that I had plenty to get where I was going and back. I even brought along two, five-gallon containers of gas, just in case. I also brought along as much water.

I knew a lot about the desert, living in the environment all my life. I knew the dangers and learned to be respectful of this rugged environment. I've seen it get ice cold with several inches of snow on the ground and I've seen it more than 120 degrees and bone dry.

The winds could blow as hard as anywhere on earth. I've seen miniature tornadoes and lighting storms that would send slivers of electricity to the ground. Violent downpours that would fill up dry riverbeds in an instant with a wall of water, carrying away anything in its path.

I stopped the car and turned off the engine and got out. I could almost hear the dark silence. A coyote howled somewhere in the distance, while a gentle wind blew. Clear, icy-cold stars hung overhead, the dark distant mountains seemed like ghosts and the desert floor were in bad need of sweeping.

I walked for several miles from the only man-made object in the area. It looked like a huge dead animal with the moonlight reflecting off the chrome. I made my way along the dry bed, making sure I made enough noise for any snakes.

I stretched my back that had cramped up from the drive. It was about seventy miles back to the freeway and the gas station. Yesterday, I made sure someone knew where I was going at the ranger station and the National Park headquarters, just in case.

My cousin worked as a park interpreter for the summer season. He was working when I stopped by, giving a lecture to a group of tourists, who gathered around him. He was describing desert life and was about to show a slide show.

I sat through it, even though I have seen it dozens of times. After he was done he held an informal question and answer period then the group went off on a short nature hike. He saw me and smiled, a little embarrassed. He was confident and outgoing. When we were kids he was usually the leader of the group of kids that hung around our neighborhood.

When all the people had drifted away, I joined him and we talked beneath the desert moon until late. We went to his government trailer and I slumped onto the uncomfortable couch. He offered me the bed, but I told him I was going to rough it the next few days anyway, I might as well start now. We talked about where I was going and he recommended several places to go and where the springs were. He loved to hunt and he had been where I was going to go several times, on his days off.

He hunted Javelina with a bow and arrow when it was in season. He would also drive up to the White Mountains and hunt deer or pheasant or wild turkeys. He was not against guns. He just thought it was more of a challenge with a bow. I didn't hunt at all. The only shots I took of animals were with my camera.

Somehow hunting with a bow and arrow didn't seem as bad. It wasn't as if some idiot with an assault rifle mowing down animals left and right.

That was last night. Now I drove a little further before I decided to camp for the night. I found a suitable place at the edge of a dry wash. I set up the sleeping bag in the back of the truck, lying on a thick foam mattress. I adjusted the box of food around as well as the box with the propane stove and lantern. I locked the front of the cab out of habit and then crawled into the warm summer bag. Being in the truck, I didn't worry about snakes or tarantulas.

A coyote bayed in the night off to my left and I heard something crash in the bushes in the same general direction. I nibbled on some cookies, making sure I did not leave out any exposed food for the animals to get to. I wasn't very hungry and didn't want to get into my main food supply. I lay back and looked up into the bright starry night. It was so bright and clear with a half moon, on its way down toward the western horizon. It seemed so quiet, I could almost make out the lights of an airplane that streaked across the sky 35,000 feet above me.

A meteor streaked its way across the sky, only to burn up before hitting the ground. With clear, dry air, the desert is a great place to see meteor showers. I used to daydream that I could travel among the stars in a spacecraft. I wasn't a Trekkie or anything like that, but traveling through the universe always fascinated me.

Another coyote called out in the opposite direction from the first. I knew that were bobcats and even mountain lions in the hills. It was a long time before I fell asleep. I awoke suddenly and didn't know what time it was. The moon had gone down and I knew from experience that it was almost dawn.

I fell asleep again and when I awoke again, the sun was about to crest the mountains to the east. It was already threatening to be a hot day. I've been in this kind of heat before so I did not worry. I knew that I could pace myself and I had plenty of water and gas and food. If anything did go wrong, my cousin knew where to search. I told him exactly where I was going.

I got up and shook out the sleeping bag. I doubled check my boots before I put them on for any unwanted surprises. I checked the cab of the truck and heard no hissing or rattling.

I made myself some breakfast, boiling the water and cooking oatmeal. Food always seemed to taste a lot better on a camping trip.

I rechecked the map and started the car and drove to a point I had marked. The air grew hotter and dryer as the morning progressed. There was no wind or any clouds in the bright blue sky. I wore a broad brim hat to cover my face and white clothing.

About mid-afternoon I stopped the truck at the base of rugged hills. The road was nothing more than a wide trail now but with four-wheel drive, I did not worry. I looked up at the reddish brown boulders that dotted the hills. My imagination took off and I thought I saw a tribe of Apaches behind the boulder, waiting for me. I strapped on a fishing knife to my waist, feeling like John Wayne in some long ago western.

I decided to drive a little further then stopped again. I decided to climb into the hills above me. I brought along a daypack and stuffed several bottles of water, a snakebite kit and my camera in it. I adjusted the pack on my back and locked the truck.

I started to climb a slight incline to the base of the hills about a mile away. As I came to a steeper incline, rocks cascaded down the slope as my foot dislodged them. I was sweating profusely now as I stopped and looked back at my truck in the distant. It seemed to wait there in loyal obedience.

I went on climbing higher now toward a craggy saddle perched between two peaks. Finally, I crested the ridge and looked down at a narrow ravine that led further into the mountains.

I stopped and looked at the map, but I didn't see the ravine represented on the map. I looked up at the sun and debated what to do. My curiosity wanted to find out where this ravine ended. I had plenty of time with no fixed destination.

I walked into the ravine now flanked on both sides by the dry, dusty slopes of the two peaks. The ravine went further than I thought. I could not see the end, since it curved and snaked its way. I decided to go back and wait for the morning when I would have more daylight.

When I got back to the truck, I started to make camp there. I set up the tent and the propane stove. I was very hungry now and made one of the freeze dry dinners. I also boiled some water and had some rice with it. I also brought along plenty of fruit.

I felt better now after I ate and sat in a beach chair in the back of the truck and watched the setting sun. I glanced up at the hills I was climbing in earlier and thought I saw a flash of light. I peered into the binoculars at the spot, straining but didn't see it again.

I laid the sleeping bag out in the tent and lit the lantern. It fizzled and ignited and the dark desert faded away just a little. I wasn't planning to stay up very long. I felt tired from the heat and the hiking. I snuggled into the bag since the desert was notorious for being cold at night.

I turned on the portable radio to pick up the Dodger game from L.A. It came in a lot better when the sun went down. They were playing the Cubs. It was nice to hear another human voice, even if it was Vince Sculley's more than four hundred miles away. I fell asleep sometime during the game. I brought an extra set of batteries for the radio and the flashlight, just in case.

I woke and the sun was still about an hour from rising. The moon had already taken its plunge into the dark mountains, leaving the black night filled with clusters of bright pencil point stars. It seemed as if I was floating in space and not on the planet.

I threw off the bag and felt the chill, not believing that it would be more than a hundred degrees in a few hours. I looked up at the hills that I would be going in the morning and I thought I saw a flicker of light. Maybe a star had fallen from the sky and landed on the mountain. I trained the binoculars on the spot for a long time but didn't see the light again. I looked a little longer with the binoculars but still saw nothing. I lay back down and waited for morning.

I woke again and saw the warm grayness of dawn. I got dressed, putting on my shorts and buckling the knife to my waist again. I made sure the water bottles were in the daypack and secured the camera strap around my shoulder. I ate a quick breakfast of cereal with powdered milk. It did not taste good and I ended up tossing half of it.

After putting some fruit in the pack, I started off anxious to get started. I got to where I was yesterday and stopped to rest. I looked into the narrow ravine and looked back at the truck, then across the wide expanse toward the distant mountains to the east. I rested a little longer then continued. The ravine got so narrow I thought it would end. Several times I had to turn sideways to get through.

The ravine opened up a little then turned into a narrow valley. The slope of the mountainside still rose sharply on both sides. After another mile, the valley became a narrow ravine again. I stopped in the sandy dry bed and saw footprints. I wasn't expecting to see signs of anyone this far from anywhere.

I checked my knife again for peace of mind and made my way through another narrow of the ravine. The ravine opened up into a wide basin and then to my surprised it ended. I looked up seeing smoke spewing out from a cave etched out of the wall of one side of the cliffs.

The cliff was almost vertical and there were primitive homemade ladders that hung from one cave down unto another lower cave. A narrow footpath that snaked its way up diagonally connected the caves.

The silence was deafening broken only by a cascade of pebbles that fell to my right. I looked up and saw a figure standing on a path above me directly in the bright sun. I shielded the sun from my eyes and angled myself to get a better look and saw a brutish man in his mid-twenties. He wore a thick bushy beard and wild unruly black hair, but it was his eyes that I noticed. They were eyes of a wild man, even like an animal's eyes.

He cradled an old rifle in his arms and suddenly almost as if coming out of a trance he started yelling in the directions of the caves. Several figures spewed out of the upper caves like ants escaping a disturbed anthill. I could barely move and when I finally did, I heard rather felt the violent thud on my head and then blackness.

I do not know how long I was out, but when I finally woke, I was in a dark cave. When my eyes adjusted, a woman leaned over me. She looked much older than she really was. Her dirty blonde hair hung with a limp across her weathered beaten face. She applied a wet cloth to my head, the sudden coldness a welcome shock to the throbbing in my head.

I tried to speak but my throat felt like dry sandpaper. I looked around and saw another female just beyond my blurring vision.

"So, he's awake now is he?" a voice boomed out of the blurry darkness. "I said is he awake?" the voice said again, angrier now.

"Yes. Can't you see that for yourself," the female voice said.

A slap echoed across the cave and the woman disappeared from view.

The man came into focus and stood in front of me. He looked like an older version of the man outside. Unruly unwashed black hair crowned his head, framed by a thick scraggly beard. The beard looked as if attacked by a knife in places. The man had the same crazy eyes as the other.

The woman came back into view adjusting the towel on my head. She did not look at me as the strange man suddenly grabbed her by the arm. She yanked her arm away glaring at him.

"It looks like you're staying here a while," the man said with a grunt.

"What?" I asked in fear.

"You better get used to this place boy," the man summarized.

"You can bet your bottom dollar we ain't going to let you go. Of course we can kill you, but then again you look strong enough to do chores."

"Why?"

It was all I could manage to say. I knew I needed my head clear if I wanted to get out of here.

"Who knows," he said with a grin. "Maybe you'll like it here. We even have women. Of course that was my woman you just saw. If you mess with her, I'll cut your balls off and feed them to you," he seethed going from friendly to anger almost at the same moment. "And my boy has a bitch too. Pretty redhead thing. Same goes for her. Mess with her and you're dead," he added softly, his mouth close to my ear. His breath was putrid like rotting flesh.

"Where am I?" I asked.

I tried to get up, but the strong hand firmly pushed my shoulder back down.

"Better get some rest boy," he said his voice rising. "We'll work you hard when you come around. Don't want you lagging around here and expect us to feed you like this is some kind of fucking hotel. Put you to work in a day or two."

He grumbled as if it was my fault that they knocked me on my head.

I closed my eyes hoping he would go away but he didn't. I opened them sometime later and saw him sitting there looking off somewhere into space.

I tried to sleep and finally nodded off to the sound of his lip smacking. When I woke it was dark and the only sounds were the crackling of the fire somewhere in the distance. I lay there listening to the crickets occasionally chirping outside the cave. It was so dark that it soothed my throbbing head, so quiet that there was ringing in my ears. I dared not to move for fear of disturbing the silence.

I woke again later in the night and at first I didn't remember where I was. I thought I was back at the truck but reality set in. The old man seemed to be an illusion that stayed in my dreams. The woman was in my dreams as well but she looked both fearful and fearing, her animal eyes constantly moving. For some reason I didn't fear the younger man even though he carried the rifle. Maybe the old man had a gun as well.

I didn't know how many of them there was. I heard about transients living in the desert, gangs of dropouts who shun society.

I tried to sleep again, but the pain kept me from slumber. A momentary panic attack forced me to get up suddenly but a rocket of pain shot through my head and I was forced to lie back down.

I didn't sense anyone else around me. It still was so pitch black I could not see anything except for the reddish glow of the embers from the dying fire. After staring I thought I saw the entrance to the cave since it was a different shade of blackness. I laid back down trying to gather my strength, which I knew I would need to get out of here.

I finally feel back to a fitful sleep punctuated by bad nightmares. Usually I didn't remember my dreams but this dream was so vivid. I dreamed someone was chasing me but I couldn't see who it was. I just knew that I had to flee.

I suddenly woke with a start. It was light out now. I could clearly see the entrance to the cave. I was about fifty feet from the entrance. I could also see several figures move about, going from the brightness of the outside with the darkness of the cave. They moved slowly as if in a trance. I realize that they were women. There were five of them. Three of them looked to be adults while the other two seemed very young girls.

I didn't see the old man or the younger man with the rifle. I didn't know how many others there were. I only saw the five women. They went about the cave carrying things or shaking out blankets and clothes.

After a while I was able to get up but not without difficulty. The woman who tended me yesterday came over to me and looked at me with concern.

"How do you feel?" she asked.

Her voice sounded as dry as the wind.

I nodded my eyes on her all the time. Her face looked bruised and weather beaten. Only her eyes showed some kind of youth.

"Where am I?" I asked.

"You don't want to know."

"Why not?" I asked.

"Because it won't do you any good," she said in a voice that seemed to quiver with fear and frustration.

"I don't know about that. There will be people looking for me," I said more to myself. "How many people live here," I probed.

"Seven, not counting you of course," she said after a long pause.

She sounded as if she had an accent but I couldn't tell what kind.

She whispered whenever she spoke as if she was afraid they would hear her.

"What are you afraid of," I asked.

"Everything and nothing," she said.

I didn't understand what she meant but I remained quiet.

"I'm getting out of here no matter what," I said. "I just need your help getting back to my truck."

"What truck?" she asked her eyes wide with fear or was it hope.

"My pickup truck. It's parked not far here," I tried to explain.

She immediately put her fingers to my mouth.

"Don't talk about your truck anymore," she said looking around.

"Why not?"

"Just do as I say. They'll go and destroy your vehicle. Then no one will ever find you," she said, not in a threatening way, but rather in a desperate tone. "Please."

I nodded without saying anything, understanding what she meant.

She froze when the man entered the cave. He looked around letting his eyes adjust from the bright sunlight to the dark cool cave then came over to where I sat. The woman fled to another part of the cave but the man only watched her with a grin. He turned his attention to me, his eyes wild.

"Are you ready to work?" he wondered.

"No," I seethed my anger and strength returning.

"You will do as I say," he glared at me, his face glowing red with anger.

"I don't know what your game is but I leaving and going back..." I stopped remembering what the woman said. "Home."

"You're not going home," he hissed.

"Why not. You can't make me do anything," I said, fear mixed in with fury.

"You are new here and still don't understand the ways things are done. But you will," he said with a sly grin.

"I don't think so. I leaving," I said standing up.

"You're not going anywhere," he leered more dangerously.

"Wanna bet."

He glared at me, and then produced a revolver, which he pointed at me menacingly.

"I think you're going to be staying with us for a long time," he said with a crazy grin. "Either above ground or below. Take your pick."

"I don't think so. People know where I am. My cousin's a cop
with the park service. He knows exactly where I am and believe
me, when I don't show up in a day or two they will be searching," I
said trying to sound as tough as I can.

A storm of fear crossed his ancient face for a brief moment then
a crooked smile flashed in its place showing rotten teeth. He wasn't
a large man but with his wild hair and beard he looked more
threatening than he was. He looked about forty with salt and
pepper color beard and hair. He wore a dirty, dust covered denim
jacket, faded blue jeans and black cowboy boots. He also wore a
Bowie knife on his belt opposite from an ancient gun holster that
held the revolver.

"You're not going anywhere," he repeated.

"How are the two of you going to guard me at all times? Cause at
the first chance, I'll escape," I threatened, pushing my luck.

He looked at me in confusion and suspicion.

"Who said that there were two of us?"

"I just assumed. I only saw the two of you," I said probing for
details.

He looked in the direction of the woman.

"We'll tie you up at night and take your boots," he said as if only
to himself. "You won't leave without water and boots. You'll do all
the heavy work during the day. Randy will guard you," he added his
eyes closed as if in deep thought.

"I don't think so," I repeated more to boost my own courage. "I
ain't doing a thing."

"Yes you will," he said with a sneer.

I didn't answer. I wasn't going to let him play mind games with
me. I would just escape at the first opportunity. Maybe the woman
will help me, I thought.

I was glad I checked into the park headquarters. My friend will
start a search in a day or two. Providing they find my truck before
these people do. I didn't worry now and I did my best to fight off
the fears that crept into my conscious.

The man left me and I started to explore the cave. No one
stopped me as they went about their business.

The oldest woman seemed to be sewing something. She didn't
look up when I neared. I wanted to get her attention.

A young girl sat next to the woman and she glared at me as if it was my fault. She was about ten and looked as dirty and animal-like as the others. There was no telling how long these people have been here. Her face also had bruises.

The older woman snapped an order to her and the girl got up as if she was a puppet. The girl gave me a quick glance before she ran off.

I went to the opening of the large cave and looked up into the bright desert sky. It was a lot hotter out in the sun as compared to the cave. I scanned around looking for the two men. I didn't see the younger man but I saw the leader down in the bowl directly below the caves.

He was squatting by a round hole in the floor of the bowl. The hole didn't seem very deep and he put something into the hole. He made a weird gesture with his hands then took the big, thick knife and pointed it up into the sky like some kind of ritual. He brought the knife down hard, stabbing the thing that he placed into the hole.

A voice behind me startled me and I spun around to face one of the women who were speaking to me. She was younger than the other woman. Her face was also streaked with dirt; her hair caked with the dust of a thousand days in the wilderness.

Two other women came up the trail toward the cave as if they materialized out of nowhere. One was in her early twenties while the other looked to be in her mid-teens. It was hard to tell their exact ages with their dirty faces. The girl's dresses were torn and really nothing more than rags. It didn't appear that they wore undergarments either.

The newcomers smiled shyly at me until the oldest woman barked an order at them and they skittered off in different directions.

I looked back, searching for the man but he had disappeared. I started down the trail but the woman's voice stopped me.

"Don't," she snapped.

"Who's going to stop me?" I asked.

"It won't do you any good," she said in surrender. "They won't let you go."

"I'm not staying here," I said in defiance.

"They know every inch of these mountains and you don't," she said sadly. "You won't get very far."

I knew she was right.

"But you do," I probed.

She didn't say anything to that. I knew she wanted to help but I suspected the fear she felt for the men.

"You have to help me," I said. "Don't you want to leave this place? To be free. To go home."

I pleaded my case but she seemed to shiver not from any coldness but from something else.

She seemed to get angry but then her features softened. She turned away without answering and I worried that she might tell the leader but she only went back to her sewing.

The twenty-year-old came by carrying a bundle and I greeted her but she smiled and didn't speak. The front of her dress was torn; the material barely covered what needed to be covered.

I felt heat generated as she passed slowly by. She glanced back with a seductive pout. She dropped the bundle and bent over without bending her knees, exposing a smooth bare ass. She glanced back again and disappeared into the cave. I almost followed her but for some reason didn't.

Another trail snaked its way along outside of the cave and disappeared around a bend. I saw only the two trails. That one and the one that went down to the floor of the canyon. I started to explore the horizontal trail that snaked out of view when the younger man came around the bend toward me. He wore a smile and pointed the rifle at me. I turned around and went back into the cave.

I knew that I had to gather my strength. I wanted to make my move soon. I couldn't stay here too long. I knew that they would tie me up at night so I planned my escape for the day. I decided to overpower the younger man and get his rifle. I pretended that I was still sick and spent the rest of the day going out of the cave as far as I could until either the old man or the other one would point their gun at me and motion for me to go back.

The younger man smiled an idiot smile. He wore his hair long and shaggy as if never saw a comb or brush. He had the same crazy eyes as the older man and I figured them to be father and son. He acted child-like but he seemed too dangerous to be retarded.

He seemed to favor the twenty-year-old girl but he also flirted openly with the teenager. He didn't pay much attention to the youngest girl. It seemed as if he was afraid of her for some reason.

He treated me with scorn whenever he passed me. Almost like a child teasing an adult and knowing that he could get away with it.

"You touch my bitch and I'll stake you to the ant hill," he warned at least once a day. "I know where there's a flying ant hill. You ever been bite by a flying ant? I have. They don't bother me. I've been bit by everything out here, scorpions, tarantulas even a centipede?"

I glared at him and he backed away waving his rifle in a threatening manner.

The day seemed to drag along and I almost wished that I had something to do.

The oldest woman would call out that it was lunch and the two older girls would serve soup made from vegetables that they grew and a small helping of rice that came from a large bag.

I didn't know where they got the rice. If they stole it from somewhere then they would have to have a vehicle of some kind. One of the girls brought over a bowl of soup and rice to me but when she reached me, the old man slapped the food out of her hands. She slithered away back to own her meal.

"He doesn't eat until he works for it," he announced gruffly. "This isn't the Holiday Inn."

The woman was about to say something but a stern look from the man and she went back to her meal.

Randy snickered to himself as he glared at me.

They ate like savages without using utensils and wiping their mouths with their shirt sleeves. They slurped their food nosily and ate the rice with their fingers. When he had finished, the older man stood up and belched loudly. Bits of rice hung from his beard but he didn't seem to notice.

He glanced over at me then turned back to face the others as if making a grand presentation.

"See what the outside brings," he said pointing a finger at me. "Trouble, nothing but trouble. He threatens us all. He wants our women and our food. Do you want to give him your food?" he asked the youngest girl.

The girl looked up at him in terror, then over at me.

"Let's stake him to the flying ant hill," Randy said with an idiot chuckle.

He started to stand up but the older man glared over at him and Randy sat back down.

"You and your fucking ant hill," The old man said.

Randy grinned and rubbed his head.

"Let's do him," Randy said after a moment.

"We need him to work," the old man said.

"I do the work around here anyway," Randy whined. "We'll have to watch him all the time."

"Not with what I have in mind," the old man said as if comforting a lost child. "No one will have to watch him and he can do your work so you can spend more time with your women. You'd like that wouldn't you?"

"Yeah," Randy said looking at the younger two girls.

"You need to get them with child," the old man spat in anger in the direction of the youngest girl. "It was bad luck with my women. We need to bear more women here not more males."

"Yeah," Randy repeated again leering at the two youngest girls.

They didn't show any emotion but I guessed that they were in some kind of trance.

"Finish your meals bitches, then finish your chores," the old man said, then spat again.

The women fumbled with their dishes and went back to their chores in obedient silence.

The old man came over to me and pointed the gun in my face.

"Last day to fuck around. Tomorrow we put you to work."

"Doing what?" I asked.

"Building your new home, that's what," he said with a grin and spat again.

"Building what?"

"Do I have to repeat myself? We're going to put you in your own place. You can't stay here in the cave."

"Where," I asked looking around the cave.

"Don't ask no stupid questions," he snapped. "You'll find out soon enough. You better get your rest cause you'll need it tomorrow," he warned then walked away."

The rest of the day dragged by slowly and even the cool of the cave grew warm and uncomfortable. No one talked to me or even came near me. I went outside but this time no one tried to stop me. It was too hot so I went back to the cave.

The woman gave me some water but I was very hungry now. Being the summer, the sun didn't set until late. Everyone gathered around the fire, which signaled that it was dinnertime. No one said anything or made any signal.

They sat around the fire as if in some kind of trance, heads bowed, eyes shut. Then suddenly as if an alarm went off in their heads at the same time, they became animated and the woman began to prepare the meal.

"I need something to eat or I won't be able to work," I said taking a chance with the old man.

He said nothing to this as he chewed on a piece of jack rabbit.

On one of my walks away from the cave I noticed that they had a pen full of about a dozen jackrabbits and chickens. The rabbits probably multiplied quickly so they had an infinite supply of meat and eggs.

"I have plenty of food and supplies back in my car. It's down the canyon west of here," I said not caring if they searched the vehicle or not.

He didn't say anything as he gnawed on the bone. He spat on the ground and looked at me.

"Already took care of your car," he said with a satisfying grin. "We ain't stupid despite what you might think. I knew you had to come in some kind of vehicle."

"What about some food," I demanded feeling sick about the car.

"Oh, quit whining like a female," he grumbled. "Louise here will fix you up something after she's done eating. Now let me be."

I felt glad about the food but depressed about the car. I hoped Jerry would start looking for me soon, but without my car being visible it would be much harder to find me. Maybe he could tell from the tracks. I told him exactly where I was going, but it will be several days before they miss me at work and they will certainly call Jerry. I might be dead by then. I wondered where they put the car.

I felt alone and hungry when the teenager brought some food over to me like I was a dangerous animal in a cage. She gave me a can of pears, which I had in the car. I knew then they were at the car. I began to eat like they did, like animals attacking their food.

"What's your name," I asked the girl who stood there staring at me.

She didn't answer and backed away and rejoined the others.

The cave felt hot even when the sun had gone down. The campfire wasn't large but it still silhouetted the group as they talked among themselves. It was the men who talked mostly while the women nodded or shook their heads.

Randy grinned his idiot grin and made their horrible chuckling sound. He draped his arms around the twenty-year-old, fondling her and kissing her.

The older man talked on while Randy stood up and half dragged the girl toward the back of the cave and some privacy. I could hear him panting and groaning in the darkness.

The older man sat staring into the fire, his face an embodiment of evil by the redness of the fire and the blackness of the night. The two younger girls sat there hugging each other while the man took the two older women with him to another part of the cave.

I laid there listening to the moans and groans. I thought of running outside and wondering why they didn't tie me up. Did they just forget? Where could I go in the night without a flashlight? It took some time to fall asleep. When I woke I could see the gray of the warm and dry dawn. I looked over at the three bundles across the cave.

The older man and the two women had a sheet over them, while Randy and the girl lay together. Everyone was naked.

I stood up without a word, keeping an eye on both groups. I moved slowly toward the mouth of the cave when the voice stopped me.

"I wouldn't try it boy," the old gruff voice said. "I got my sights on your brains right now."

I turned around and saw him point the pistol at me.

"Need to take a leak," I said with anger.

Randy was standing up, putting on his pants and reaching for his rifle at the same time. He came over and stuck the rifle into my ribs.

"Let blow him away now. He's too much trouble," he said playing with his belt buckle.

The older man also put his pants on.

"Naw, I got plans for him," the old man said. "Take him out so he could take his leak. And watch him. Come on girls and get breakfast going," he yelled to the girls.

They started scrambling out of the bedrolls and dressing quickly. Randy guided me out to the area where the general toilet was. It smelled horrible but no one else seemed bothered by the smell. When I was done he pushed me back to the cave where he tied me up.

They ate noisily, grunting and belching as if caveman from thousands of years ago. When they finished, the same girl who fed me last night came over with a small helping of eggs and rice. She did not look at me as I struggled to eat with my hands tied.

The woman began with their daily chores, which they seemed to do automatically as if robots. I watched the youngest feed and take care of the chickens and rabbits. She picked up one rabbit by the neck and as it kicked for freedom, she held it tightly to her cheek.

"Elizabeth," the oldest woman called from the cave.

For a moment the girl wouldn't release the rabbit but when her name was called a second time, she seemed to come out of a trance. She set the rabbit back in the pen and ran back to the cave.

I could see Randy in the distance grinning at me and waving the rifle around as if I should know he would always be watching. I went back into the cave where it was cooler. The older man was fondling the teenager by the fire as I came in. He didn't seem to notice me as he fondled her breasts and kissed her hard. He began to force himself on her and I went to the back of the cave and sat down.

I pushed my head against the cool wall of the cave. Feeling thirsty I got up and skimmed my way past the lovers and made my way to the small spring outside the cave.

There were several palm trees surrounding the spring. They also had a small garden which two of the girls tended to regularity. I took a few sips of the cool, dirty water when the voice behind me spoke.

"Follow me," the old man spoke. He looked angry, his eyes aflame with desert emotion.

"Where?"

"Don't ask no stupid question," he said yanking me up roughly with his strong hands. "Just come on."

He walked behind me on a trail away from the cave. The trail dropped down into a smaller narrow canyon similar to the one I walked up the other day. How many days as it been, I thought, looking up at the bright morning sun.

We came to a fork in the canyon. A larger canyon continued on while a smaller canyon forked off to the right. He pushed me to the right and we walked several hundred yards when the canyon narrowed further then stopped altogether. It was shaped like a keyhole, the wall narrowing then opening up into a round basin. A shovel stuck out in the middle of the basin.

"Dig," the old man said.

"Dig what?" I asked.

"Another question? Don't asked stupid questions. Just dig till you see some china men," he snorted.

I looked at him quizzically.

"I thought you college boys were so smart," he said with a spit. "You are digging your prison see. Fill in this gap here and you have yourself your own pen. There's a trail that runs along up there. The girls will drop a ladder down for you when we need some work done. This way we don't have to keep an eye on you."

He grinned like it was the best idea. He spat again as I tried to control my fear.

"I'll die in there," I whined.

"Don't be a stupid ass," he said. "You ain't going to die. We'll feed you some. Providing you work for it. Of course when the summer flash floods come, you just might drown. And even if you do die, we have your grave already dug. Convenient huh?" He laughed a gruff laugh at his joke.

I knew I had to make my escape before I filled in the gap.

"Too much trouble to keep an eye out for you back at the cave. Sides, we need the privacy," he chuckled. "Besides one of those bitches might try and free you."

"I thought I was going to work," I said.

"You will. We'll drop things down for you to do. And when we need something done elsewhere, we'll escort you. We can't have you hanging around free like. You might try for our bitches. Now start digging," he cursed. When I didn't move, he produced his pistol.

I grabbed the handle of the shovel, knowing I would have to make my move soon. I dug slowly filling the gap slowly. He stood by and waited. I was going to wait until he lowered his gun. After a moment his attention started to drift and I got into position.

I moved closer to him and when the time was right I threw a shovel full of dirt at his face.

He threw his hands up to protect himself but it was too late. Momentarily blinded, I swung the shovel catching him across the side of the head. I heard the sickening thud but I didn't stop swinging, harder and harder until he fell to the ground.

He dropped the gun and I picked it up checking to see if it was loaded. It wasn't. There wasn't even a firing pin.

He lay on the ground motionless and I checked his pulse and felt none. I felt excited and scared as I looked around expecting the younger man. Wet with sweat, my hands shook as I held the empty gun.

Would Randy know that the old man's gun didn't have any bullets, I wondered? I suspected he knew. I made my way back along the canyon floor coming to where the canyon merged with the other larger canyon. I knew the caves were just ahead and I kept an eye on the cliff above me.

When I neared the caves I heard yelling and screaming.

"Oh no, Oh no," Randy screamed hysterically. "It's not supposed to be. He killed him. He killed him."

He came up from one of the trails that led along the cliff walls. My guess was that he found the body.

I wished that I had bullets for the gun but I didn't and I couldn't dwell on that. I thought about heading back in the direction of the car but I didn't know what happened to it and I was a little confused on the direction.

I made my way up the cliff to where the trail to the cave was. I did not want to be below him in case he had bullets in the rifle. I moved away from the caves thinking the women might have a gun as well. I didn't quite trust them either.

I head along the trail that snaked around a peak and dropped over a saddle separated two small peaks. I decided to hide and wait until dark. I knew I had to go back and get some water and the rest of my stuff. I found a place to hide in the crevice among some boulders, which allowed me to see if someone came into view.

The sun beat down on me as if it was a boxer pummeling a down opponent. I finally moved when the sun sank just below the distant hills and the air cooled a little.

Sunsets in the desert are usually spectacular and this one was not any different but I wasn't in the mood to watch beautiful sunsets. I rested my eyes and somehow fell asleep in the uncomfortable position. When I woke it was dark. I knew I couldn't go another day without food and water.

I made my way in the dark back toward the caves. When I rounded the bend I saw the unnatural evil glow of the fire in the cave. I knew that they couldn't see me even if they were there on the lip of the cave. I saw several bodies lying near the fire and one sitting in a lotus position on the lip of the mouth.

It was Randy and he was holding his rifle tightly. He kept spinning his head from side to side as if looking for something.

I came as close as I could without being seen. I could hear the soft snoring of the women. One tossed in her sleep and I saw Randy looked back at her as if it was a major intrusion on his vigil. He sat Indian style as I crept slowly to his side. I could tell he was nervous and that was to my advantage.

A coyote sang his lonely song in the night and I could see him jumped. In an instant Randy jumped up and faced in my direction, his rifle pointed at my mid-section. I crouched down and tried not to breathe. The animals howling continue and Randy seemed to relax and sat back down on his legs.

He was now facing me and I thought about retreating and circling around. After a while he turned back to his original position facing into the dark night.

I stood up and walked silently toward him. It was almost as if I was a ghost I walked so quietly. My eyes bored into him as I brought the revolver up and slammed it into the back of his head. With a dull moan he slumped over and was silent. I waited for a moment taking a deep breath, then felt for a pulse and found a weak one.

"The other?" the voice snapped me out of my trance and I spun around expecting a blow.

The older woman had been standing there all this time and I had thought she would have warned Randy but she didn't.

"The other?" she asked again in her dry desert voice.

"Dead," I heard myself say, but it didn't sound like my voice.

She seemed to collapse like a balloon being deflated of air. She leaned against the wall of the cave with one hand. It looked as if she was going to be sick if it wasn't for the small grin she wore. She started shivering but I knew she wasn't cold since it was a warm night.

The fire added to the heat and I realized that I was drenched with sweat. The other four girls woke as if wind-up toys and they came toward Randy's prone body.

"Is he..." asked the twenty-year-old, brushing her hair from her face and looking around.

"So he says," said the older woman.

The girls looked at me as if they were waiting for me to give orders.

I picked up the rifle and checked it and not to my surprise I saw that it was also empty. I check Randy's pockets and found nothing.

"There were no bullets," the older woman said. "We used them up long ago to kill game."

"What do you eat?"

"Just what we grow and the rabbits occasionally and a chicken on special occasion. Sometimes we snare things," the woman said.

"Who were they?" I asking pointing to Randy who wasn't dead yet. I wondered what to do with him. I looked around for some rope to tie him up.

"Al was my brother," she whispered. "Randy was just a friend of his."

I froze as if expecting her to charge me with a knife but she didn't seem to care.

"I sorry. I didn't know."

"Not your fault. I would have done the same thing. In fact, I wanted to kill him many times myself."

"Why?" I asked confused. "He's your brother."

"He was also my tormentor as well as my lover," she spat. It seemed she had emotion in her for the first time in a long time.

"Your..."

"Yeah. Angie there, she's our daughter. Of course that didn't stop him from..." She put her hand to her mouth as if the enormity of it all finally made an impression on her. "He already killed off several of our sons. He left Randy alone since he wasn't a threat to anyone. He was soft in the head you know," she said with a warm look at Randy.

I watched her as she spoke.

"Katie is Randy's girlfriend," she introduced the twenty-year-old girl.

The girl looked at me with fear and suspicion. She didn't go to Randy or even know that he was lying there.

I bent over to check on him again.

"Kill him," said the older woman in a calm voice.

"What?"

"If you don't, I will," she said coldly.

When I didn't move, she went over and pulled the Bowie knife from the sleeping bag and came back right at me. I backed up in defense but she passed me and went over to Randy and neatly cut his throat.

I stepped back in shock as she wiped the blade calmly and put it back in its sheath.

"What did you do that for?" I shouted but she only walked back to her sleeping bag and sat down as if the weight of a thousand lifetimes had lifted from her shoulders.

"I said why..."

"If I didn't, then she would have," the woman said not specifying who 'she' was. The other girls nodded weakly and joined the woman by the fire.

I wanted to sleep but I was afraid the woman would cut my throat. I thought about taking the knife away. I was afraid Randy would get up and kill me, saying it was all a joke.

I was even afraid the older man would come into the cave with his jack-o-lantern grin and waving a shovel at me. I rubbed my eyes with fatigue and sat down by a rock near the fire.

I woke suddenly and looking around. A rocket of fear shot through me. Was that all a dream? Maybe Randy and the old man weren't dead after all? The women were lying next to the fire and soft snoring emitted from them.

I got up and looked at Randy who still lay on his side, black liquid lay in a pool near his head. I rubbed my throat and went back to the fire that was now only a glow of embers. I relaxed and leaned back against the wall.

The figure came over and sat next to me. For a second, I panicked reaching for the empty gun but the girl soothed my fears as she cuddled up next to me. I realized she didn't have a knife so she wasn't going to cut my throat. It took another moment to realize that she had nothing on.

She began to kiss my face and chest then settling on my lips. She unbuttoned my jeans and began oral sex. I leaned back and enjoyed it and when she was done I took my clothes off and we had hot, passionate sex until the sun came up.

The morning heat and the sex made me feel weak but satisfied. The women got up and started with their chores as if nothing had happened. I drummed up my energy and dragged Randy's body away from the mouth of the cave.

I dragged him to where the older man still lay and buried both of them. The old man was right. I was digging a hole. I smiled at this and even allowed myself to kick the corpse's body in the head. Of course they didn't feel it but it made me feel better.

When I finished, I returned to the cave. The women were busy with their chores. I went down to the bowl below the caves and pulled back a small tarp that covered a hole. I had taken the Bowie knife from the woman earlier and checked the object that lay on the bottom of the hole. She had given up the knife as if expecting me to ask for it. The object looked the same and I put the tarp back and went back to the cave satisfied.

Several weeks later I went for a walk down the canyon, back toward where I left my car. I made written notes of the route to the truck. I made it to my car and was surprise that it was still sitting there as if it was waiting for me.

I hid the vehicle with bushes and when I finished, I looked out across the wide expense of the desert. Above me, a silver trail of a jet slowly crossed the sky. I felt a moment of melancholy but then it passed and I turned and went back to the cave to my women.

They were my women now, even the 11-year-old. We all slept together like a family now. It took time but the girls were smiling now and laughter echoed off the ancient cave walls. I think the twenty-year-old girl is pregnant. I sure hope it's a girl.

The End

THE SOUND OF FURY

The Sound looked as rough as he had ever seen it. The oppressive gray skies grew darker as inconsistent drops of rain tap-danced on the deck of the small fishing boat. Wind-blown waves hammered the boat as it bobbed in the emerald green water. Turner bundled himself deeper into his Navy pea coat, steering the thirty-five-foot boat to a sheltered cove off Bainbridge Island near Seattle. He stared at the warm yellow lights of the expensive homes that dotted the island.

He shut down the engines and went out onto the bow to drop the anchor. When he was sure that the line was secured, he went below. What he saw annoyed him.

The boy ate a candy bar and watched something on the small portable TV. Except for a small light above the bunk, the television's bluish tint illuminated the cabin. The boy's older cousin slept on the bunk to the right.

An empty bottle of soda lay next to the TV. The door of the small refrigerator lay partially open, exposing a quart of milk and a six-pack of beer, minus three cans.

"Don't you see the door is open?" Turner asked.

The boy did not seem to hear, his attention absorbed on the bluish light.

"Light's out for tonight," Turner said, turning off the television.

"Hey."

"Hey, nothing," Turner said. "It's getting late and you're wasting the battery watching that junk."

"My dad's paying you for this charter and we didn't even catch anything," the boy said.

"It's still my boat and what I say goes," Turner said. "You can go home in a few days and watch TV all you want. Tomorrow we're getting up early and going fishing. That's what you're paying me for" He checked the level of the batteries on the gauges and grimaced.

The boy looked at the black man as if he was insane, then crawled into his sleeping bag on the bunk opposite his cousin. He listened to the wind as it lashed against the tiny porthole.

The rain above sounded like thousands of tiny footsteps tap dancing on the deck above. The swells gently rocked the boat, straining the anchor line that squealed with the tension.

****

Even though it was still very dark and cold, Turner gladly shook the two boys awake. Eric, a gentle looking twelve-year-old, jumped up with a start, not knowing where he was for a moment.

Turner himself looked as if he had not slept all night, which he did not. He held a steaming cup of coffee in one hand while he tried to wake Gary, Eric's seventeen-year-old cousin. Gary moaned, but didn't get up.

"Come on, boy," Turner said. "The fish are waiting for us."

"I don't feel so good," Gary moaned.

He turned slowly in his sleeping bag.

"Come on."

"Really, man. I didn't sleep much last night. Didn't you hear me in the can?"

"Yeah, I heard you," Turner said. "You're breaking my heart. Come on. I don't want you bitching that you didn't get your money's worth."

Eric pulled on his jeans, uncomfortable about dressing in front of the black man. He buttoned up a flannel shirt, and then pulled a heavy wool sweater over the thermal underwear he slept in. Turner handed him a yellow rain coat, then went topside.

Two bowls of oatmeal were sitting on the table, steam rising from them like gray volcanoes. The boy poured milk in the bowl and added sugar and ate the hot cereal quickly. When he finished, he hurried up the ladder onto the deck eager for adventure.

Turner pulled up the anchor and started the engines with the turn of the key. The diesels sputtered to life and the black man spun the chrome wheel around, pointing the boat northward.

Eric grabbed his pole from its holder and studied the artificial green squid.

"Throw it out when I say so," Turner said.

The boy threw the line out as far as he could and with the downrigger in place he trolled for a while. The sky became lighter and the shoreline grew more visible. Turner threw in another line set up with the other down rigger and went back to the wheel. They fished most of the day, coasting slowly up and down the Sound.

After a while, Turner saw Eric was not getting any bites and he stopped the engine. The air was razor cold but the rain stopped and the wind died down. Eric wished he had brought along his wool-lined gloves.

The black man came back to the chair and sat next to him.

"Reel in the line and we can try some bottom fishing if you want," he said.

He handed the boy another pole. Eric baited the hook with a live anchovy from the bait tank in the back, dropped it to the bottom, then clicked the bail over. He sat down, balancing the pole with his fingers.

"How long have you had this boat?" Eric said.

He looked at the older man with his salt and pepper hair framing his dark, leathery face.

"It was my daddy's," Turner said. "He bought it when I was in college. He always wanted a boat. He always saw the rich white... rich... other people towing their boats to the Sound or to lakes. He saved his money like crazy, even taking another job. When a guy at work offered to sell his, my daddy jumped at the chance. Not too many black fishing boat captains around."

Eric did not answer. He always felt uncomfortable talking about race to black people.

"So you went to college?" the boy asked.

"Surprised?" Turner snapped.

He looked at the boy but he didn't see any malice in the child's face.

"For two years. I came home when my daddy died," Turner said.

"How did he die?" Eric asked.

Turner did not speak for a long time and Eric thought he wasn't going to answer. He really did not want to pry.

"A group of white kids hanging around the marina started taunting him. Calling him names. This was in the 70s. My old man was a fighter. He wasn't about to take any shit from some snot nose little crac..." Turner stopped to compose himself, his black eyes aflame with anger.

"One night a carload of them came down to the marina. My old man was working late on the boat. They started to call him names, taunting him and he responded. They beat him with baseball bats and fists." Turner got up and looked out at the water before he continued.

"He lived for several weeks, but he was little more than a vegetable."

Eric did not say anything. He wished he hadn't asked the black man about his father.

"I guess your cousin isn't coming up," Turner said.

Eric did not say anything glad the conversation had shifted. He could not shake the horrible image of someone being beaten to death. He shuddered and reeled up the line.

"Are you cold, boy?"

"No," Eric said. He reeled his line up and saw that his bait was gone.

"Cause I have an extra sweater in the cabin."

"No. I'm fine."

"Your mother will skin me alive if you catch a cold."

"I'm fine," Eric insisted.

He rebaited the hook and threw the line out again. When he guessed the bait was deep enough he clicked the bail over.

"You ever see a ghost?" Eric asked.

"What you mean by a ghost?" Turner said.

"A ghost. You know what a ghost is," Eric said.

"You mean like Casper the ghost or Ghost Busters? No, but I do believe in spirits."

"What's the difference?" Eric asked.

"Ghosts, I always visualize as dudes with white sheets and I try to stay away from them," Turner said. He laughed at the joke but the boy didn't seem to get the humor.

"The Suquamish Indians believed that if you're sick, it was because the spirits had stolen your soul," Turner said. "They believed that animals, birds, fishes and even inanimate objects possessed spirits. There's an Indian burial ground over there near that point. Once I saw what looked like someone rowing a canoe just over there." Turner pointed towards a thickly wooded area on the shore.

"A canoe?" Eric asked.

"A large wooden canoe with several men rowing it and they were chanting an old Indian song. When I got closer they were gone."

"What was it?"

"I don't know. Spirits I guess," Turner said.

"So these spirits were rowing a canoe?" Eric said. "That's so cool. Sounds like a ghost story to me." He studied the black man who focused his steady gaze on the distant shore. Eric followed his gaze and stared at the densely wooded land.

Suddenly there was a tug on the line that startled Eric, who almost dropped the pole. The boy reeled in the line careful not to allow any slack. He stopped reeling and felt the line with his finger and realized that there wasn't anything on the hook.

"Damn it," he cursed.

Turner was still staring across the water as the boy reeled the line all the way in. He saw the bait was gone. He got another anchovy, baited the hook and threw the line out again.

"Ever see a ghost up close?" Eric asked.

Turner acted as if he was stabbed by the question. "I went over there one day. Can't get there but by boat. Walked around the place. Made my skin crawl. Never felt so uncomfortable in my life."

"Uncomfortable?"

"Yeah, uncomfortable. It wasn't like I was scared or anything. Just an uneasy feeling about the place. Uncomfortable is the way I would put it."

"Did you see anything?"

"A totem pole near a grave. A tall one with eagle faces and anchors and beaver faces."

"A grave?" Eric asked.

"More like a large mound with rocks placed on it. The Suquamish sometimes buried their dead in canoes."

"Let's go over there tonight," Eric said.

Turner stood up and shook his head. "No sireee. You're not getting me to go over there again."

"Come on. It would cheer Gary up to get off the boat and walk around. We can make a fire on the beach," Eric pleaded.

"No. Your mother wouldn't go for that."

"She wouldn't know. Anyway, we paid for this charter."

"Fishing is what you paid for. This isn't a ghost hunting expedition. So forget it."

"You're chicken," Eric said.

"Don't talk that way boy. That's childish," Turner said.

Eric did not want to admit that he was spoiled but it bothered him when he didn't get his way.

"Do you want to move or stay here a bit longer?" Turner asked. He reeled up the line from the other pole.

Eric did not say anything. He was still angry about wanting to see a ghost.

Turner went below to check on the other boy who moaned and groaned. Gary sat on the bed with his head bent over between his knees.

"Haven't got your sea legs yet, huh?" Turner said. Turner had always felt more comfortable at sea than on land. He loved to go along when his father took people out fishing. He had read everything there was about the ocean from Rachel Carson to Jacques Cousteau to Hemingway's 'Old Man and the Sea.' Out on the sea he felt free of the hatred, racism and fear.

"Get outside in the fresh air. You'll feel better," Turner said.

"Leave me alone, boy," Gary said.

Turner tensed, but said nothing and went back on deck. Suddenly he knew something was wrong. Eric had disappeared along with the small dinghy that he tied behind the boat. Turner tried to calm himself as he scanned the Sound with his binoculars. In the distance, he saw the small dinghy bobbing against the small waves.

"Damn it," Turner said.

After he pulled up the anchor, he tried several times to start the boat before it finally roared to life. He spun the wheel around and guided the boat in the same direction. Eric had gotten a good lead and Turner pushed the lever as fast as he could go. He cursed himself for putting the Merc 50 on the dinghy.

He guided the boat into a small bay. A miniature island sat several hundred yards offshore. He spotted the dinghy along the beach and maneuvered the boat as close as he could to shore. The water was clear and he could see the rocky bottom below.

With a grappling hook, he managed to snag the dinghy and tied it to the boat. He then reversed the engines and took the boat out to deeper water, where he dropped the anchor.

He got into the dinghy and guided the smaller craft toward shore. He beached the dingy and walked up the narrow beach into the dense woods. He tried to remember where the burial ground was.

He had to stop twice to get his bearings. Blackberry bushes grabbed at him and rhododendron bushes got in his way as he finally came to a clearing. The rock-strewn mound was at the far end of it.

He saw the boy lying on the ground near the mound. He was not moving and for a moment Turner started to panic. He turned the boy over and to his relief Eric opened his eyes. He sat up and rubbed the back of his head.

"My head," the boy moaned.

"What happened?"

"Someone hit me from behind," Eric said.

He tried to get up but Turner, the sea and the forest all seemed to be spinning.

"Don't try to get up. Just stay there," Turner said, looking around.

"Maybe they're still around," Eric said.

"I didn't see any other boats around and there are no roads around here," Turner said.

"Someone conked me. I didn't grow this lump by myself," Eric said.

Turner felt the boy's head, pushing aside the blonde hair.

"Ouch."

"Sorry, boy. Yeah. There's a beaut of a bump."

"Why is it okay for you to call me a boy, but not the other way around?" Eric asked.

"Cause you are a boy and I'm not," Turner said studying him.

"Can we stay on shore for the night? I can fish from shore and Gary can get off the boat," Eric asked.

"You sure are hot and bothered to see a spirit aren't you?" Turner asked. "We should get you home with that bump. Might be serious."

He looked around the meadow, helping the boy to his feet.

"I'm fine. I've had worse bruises than this," Eric said.

"Let's get back to the beach," Turner said. "I have a weird feeling about this."

When they got to the beach, they found the beached dingy but something seemed different. Turner had a strange feeling but he shook it off.

"I'll get Gary and any supplies we need and bring them back to shore. When I get back you can take the boat out a ways and fish near that small island."

"Is there anything to catch except for those damn little sharks?"
Eric whined.
"Dogfish? There are other fish, but there's mostly a lot of dogfish.
Maybe out in that kelp you can get away from them," Turner said.
"How about halibut?"
"Not around here. You have to go out in the straits by Neah Bay.
Now wait here while I get your cousin. You sure you're okay?"
Turner asked.
"Fine," Eric said.
"Stay here," Turner said.
He pushed the dingy out into the water and rowed slowly toward
the boat.
A snap of a branch startled Eric and he spun around. He didn't see
anything but he had the feeling someone was watching him. He
started to panic and thought of swimming out to the boat. He
watched Turner guide the dingy and wished that Turner would
hurry.
Another noise and he spun around. He felt a cold icy presence. It
seemed everywhere, within and outside him. The silence grew
deafening and he felt the tingle of fear. He closed his eyes and held
out his arms as if to ward off an enemy. Finally, he found his feet
and turned and ran right into the body.
He screamed as Turner wrestled with him, trying to calm him
down.
"Easy boy. You look as if you just seen a ghost," Turner said.
Eric looked at the black man and his cousin who stood behind
him.
"Feeling better?" he asked his cousin.
Gary only smiled weakly.
"The tide gets drastic in the Sound. I'll tie the dingy to a tree,"
Turner said,
"You boys get the stuff out of the boat. It's getting late."
"Is there a road around here? Maybe I can thumb back," Gary
asked.
"What a wimp. You were the one telling me what a great fisherman
you are," Eric teased.
"Yeah, on streams and lakes. I don't really care for victory at sea,"
Gary said.
"We're not even close to the ocean, you moron."
"You looked as if you were going to crap in your pants just a

minute ago," Gary said.

Both boys looked at Turner who faced the forest as if facing an army of giants.

"What's wrong?" Eric asked.

"Nothing. Hurry up with the stuff," he said.

By the time they had set up the small dome tents and unrolled the sleeping bags and made a fire it was nearly dark. The sky had cleared up, which meant a colder night. The stars blinked down at them from their icy perch.

They ate dinner in silence and when they finished, they put away the dishes and sat around the fire. Eric studied the black man's face.

"How about one of your Indian stories," Eric said.

Turner did not move, his mind elsewhere. Gary yawned, and looking bored, played with the fire with a stick. Eric moved closer to the fire feeling the heat on his legs.

"You read a lot, don't you?" Eric asked.

"What's wrong with that? Nothing wrong with expanding your mind. Better than watching those idiotic TV shows," Turner said. Suddenly he glanced up and turned toward the forest.

"What is it?" Eric asked. He squinted past the campfire into the darkness but didn't see anything.

Turner stood up and started walking toward the trees in a trance-like state.

Eric glanced at his cousin, who only shrugged and went back to the fire.

"Come on, Gary" he said.

Eric followed the black man into the woods.

"Turner?" Eric called out.

But the black man did not respond. Branches brushed the boy's face, while thorn bushes scratched his legs like prying fingers, trying to grab at him. They could see Turner just ahead of them. They came to the edge of the clearing where Turner stood with his eyes closed.

The black man seemed unaware of the boys behind him. He felt the presence of the dead spirits around him. Turner closed his eyes and felt their suffering, heard their crying, their lamentation, saw their poverty and hopelessness. He opened his eyes and they stood before him.

One wore a snake mask that opened up into a bear mask, which in

turn opened up into a third mask with a human face. Another wore
a wolf mask and held a carved bone in his hand, which he pointed
in Turner's direction.
Turner realized that the spirit wasn't pointing at him, but at the
boys he knew were behind him.
Eric glared at the darkness, sensing something, but not seeing
anything. He thought he saw movement to his right. He looked up
at Turner, who stared straight ahead as if in a trance.
Turner turned around and headed back to camp without a word.
Eric did not move, feeling a presence that seemed to hold him
there. The boy turned back to face what he could not see. He
found himself drawn to the mound before him. He saw a long
shape that hovered several feet above the ground. It was a canoe lit
by an eerie, bluish glow beneath it. It looked like a glow from a hot
flame but without the fire.
He moved closer to see what was inside, when suddenly it grew
very cold and he stopped. He heard the chanting. It was low at
first, then grew in intensity and was joined by a rattling noise. Eric
moved closer to the canoe and looked inside.
A man, wearing a wolf mask, lay on the bottom of the canoe. He
was wrapped in an Indian blanket and wore a necklace of shells and
bear claws. He appeared to be dead, but suddenly he sat up and
pointed a bleached, white bone at Eric.
Eric backed up and started to run. He ran past a dark shape that
tried to grab him but missed. He stumbled once and got up in
panic.
"Turner?" he called out.
He fought his way through the thick bushes that seemed to reach
out for him, avoiding the tall shapes of the large cedar trees.
Finally, the bushes and trees disappeared and he knew he was on
the beach. He saw the blackness of the water in front of him.
Something was wrong though. He looked up and down the beach,
but did not see the campfire. He turned back towards the forest
and felt the cold presence reach out to him. He found himself
backing up into the water. Biting cold water soaked his tennis
shoes, then his jeans. He slipped on the rocks and cut his hand on
an oyster shell.
He made his way along the beach, hoping that he was going in the
right direction.
When he rounded the point, he saw the campfire in the distance.

As he neared the fire, he saw Turner sitting there, his back to him, silhouetted against the fire. He did not turn around when the boy approached.

"Did you see your ghost?" Turner asked.

Eric turned and faced him. He could not see the eyes that sat like dark pools on an even blacker surface. The reddish glow of the fire illuminated the bridge of his nose and part of his cheek. It looked like a mask of black death.

"Yeah, I saw it. Where's Gary?" Eric asked.

"Right here, you chicken shit," Gary said, emerging from the tent. "Where did you go?"

"Didn't you see it?" Eric asked.

"See what?" the older boy asked. "You ran past me, almost knocking me down. I thought you were going to swim back to Seattle."

He was convinced that Eric was crazy.

Eric was about to retaliate when Turner spoke in a voice as old as time.

"Time to go to bed. You have a long way to go tomorrow," Turner said.

The black man faced the fire again and closed his eyes feeling the heat from the flames on his death-like black face.   "A long way to go," he repeated softly.

The End

ENDLESS DESTINATION

Just as she peeked through the dark tinted glass of the double doors, the sound of sharp metallic click made the woman jump. Another click unlocked the other set of double doors. The metallic click sounded just like that other metallic sound of so many years ago in that other place that will never leave her tormented memory. Slowly returning to the present, the well dressed, gray-hair woman again looked inside and saw a dark shadowy figure disappear from view.

Mrs. Schulz rudely ignored the elderly Hispanic janitor who wore a tight smile on his tanned face as he held the door open for her. She pushed past him leaving fingerprints on the glass and set foot onto the sterile tile, which he freshly mopped the night before.

She was alone, but she knew others would soon join her. The woman glanced down one end of the mall. Fluorescent lights slowly came on, one by one, chasing the darkness away. The shopping mall opened this early, but the individual stores would not open for several more hours. The woman enjoyed the mall at this hour. It was free of teenage kids who strolled around in menacing groups.

She adjusted her dark blue sweat pants and started walking the top floor of the two-story super mall. Once around was almost three quarters of a mile. Four times around was three miles and that was her limit.

After all, she was almost seventy. She still thought she was in good shape. How many sixty-nine-year-old women go on three-mile walks and still play several sets of tennis in the afternoon? It was a ritual, five days a week, rain or shine. Sometimes she failed to make her trek and she regretted it until the next time she came to the mall.

She walked at a steady pace along the top floor. It formed a rectangular track down one side, ending at a major department store, then back on the other side, finishing at another department store. In the center was a pair of escalators that went down to a lower floor.

The woman scanned the dark boutiques, a book store, a pet shop, another boutique, an electronic store and a travel agency.

She glanced at a poster of a Hawaii ad. A beautiful girl in a revealing bikini lay prone on a pure white beach with clear blue water behind her. The woman ignored the girl and studied the sailboat that tacked its one-dimensional way across the cardboard ocean.

She walked on, passing a music store with posters of long-hair rock stars and black rappers in threatening poses. She shook her head at these posters and went on. She knew by heart the order of each store.

She saw someone else slowly walking in the opposite direction. It was too late to avoid the short, balding, bony thin man.

"Good morning Mrs. Schulz," he said in a thick New York accent. "How are we today?"

He wore a suppressed grin on his face, framed by a narrow mustache that drooped annoyingly downwards. The grin morphed into a surprised look as if she just spat in his face.

So disgusting and animal-like, Mrs. Schulz thought. She smiled at the image of a rat wearing a stupid jogging outfit and he mistakenly thought it was a friendly smile. She kept going, feeling his penetrating rat-like eyes on her back. They were right, she thought. They were just like rats.

He was one of the early walkers. Every day he greeted her with his knowing eyes always on her and every day she ignored him. One dismal day, he went so far as to ask a simple question. She looked at him as if he was insane and walked away without giving an answer.

By now several other people walked the rectangular circuit. Some walked in the opposite direction, some walked in groups, and some walked alone.

The woman liked to walk alone, though some days Mrs. Burke would join her. Alice Burke was also a widow, but she failed to show up the last few days and Mrs. Schulz started to worry.

The woman walked at a steady pace, not speeding up or slowing down. She rounded the corner and crossed the short span to the other side. The woman ignored the department store ads and the mannequins posing in the latest fashion.

She thought back to when she was a young girl. The fashions were so different then. Covering so much and revealing very little. She had lived through more than a half century of changes in hairstyles, clothes, even language.

It seemed simpler back then. Life was a moonlight stroll in a park. Now it was loud discotheques and unfriendly bars. People seemed content with their lives, their spouses, even their jobs back then. In today's fast-food society, there were multiple career changes, multiple divorces and experimental marriages. Television shows evolved from quality well-written dramas and comedies to realty shows of inane stupidity. In the past, heroes earned respect while today, untalented celebrities are worshipped.

The shops whirred past her, dark and empty behind black spider-web gates. The woman didn't see the New York rat and she smiled at that.

As she approached the center of the mall she stopped, not wanting to, but having to. She clutched her chest in sudden panic at the sharp pain. She leaned against a pillar for support.

"Are you okay?" an accented voice said from behind.

She acted as if she didn't hear him.

"Are you...?" the voice repeated.

"Yes. I'm fine," she gasped.

As the pain slowly subsided, she felt herself breathe easier.

"You must not push yourself too hard," the Jew said with fake concern.

"I would appreciate it, if you'd mind you own business," she hissed at him.

She did not see him shrug as she took several steps on her way. He didn't see her wear her frown like a burden. The pain disappeared, but the fear and panic remained.

She continued on, but at a slower pace. She came to the department store at the far end finishing the first lap with three more laps to go. She had done this many times, but today it seemed like such a long arduous way. She was half-way around the second lap, when Mrs. Mellis caught up with her.

"Morning Agnes," Mrs. Mellis said in her slight European accent. "Pretty day. Yes?"

Even though she had lived in this country since she was a teen, the woman never lost her Eastern European accent.

"Yes. Lovely day."

"I almost decided to walk outside today, but the traffic..."

"Yes. The traffic."

"And you have to deal with those kids with their skateboards and their weird hair," the woman said.

"Yes. The kids."

"They throw things," Mrs. Mellis said. "Such rude children. How is everything at home?"

"Yes. Everything's fine. Why?"

"No reason. Just concerned... I mean now that you are alone. I mean that Robert is out on the coast and Lori is in Chicago with..."

"Please, Mrs. Mellis. Addy. I don't mean to be rude, but right now..."

She did not finish. She didn't really hate Mrs. Mellis whose father fled the pogroms of Russia. She didn't really hate any of them as much as Frank did. Except for that annoying rat-like New Yorker, who would have followed her around the mall like a gray ghost. She just didn't want to have anything to do with them. She couldn't apologize for what Frank did in the war. She was just a young girl when the war ended and she and her family moved to this country with literally nothing except their clothes, rags really. Frank, it was Franz then, was barely a teen-ager when he got caught up in Hitler's youth movement and did things, bad things to the rats. It wasn't her husband's fault when he found the wide-eyed adolescent boy and the eight other children in the farmhouse near their village. With the metallic click of his MP-40 machine gun, he simply followed the orders of the obese SS officer who sometimes touched him when others were not around.

Franz Schubert came to this country and kept his terrible secret to himself but his hatred for the rats continued to burn deeply, which his wife shared. She met him in the slums of New York more than a half a century ago. The rats were the reason their beloved country lay in ruins and why she and her husband were forced to leave. Franz would have shot more of those rats in that farmhouse if the American soldiers didn't arrive just then to capture him and severely beat him almost to death.

She loved her husband unconditionally and vowed to keep his secret and her contempt to her grave. Even her own children never knew what their father did to the Jews so many years ago.

More and more people filed into the mall now. The woman finished the second lap and started the third. Mrs. Mellis walked in silence behind her like a lost puppy, and then finally left.

"I'm going to walk outside. Too pretty of a day," Mrs. Mellis said with a wave.

The woman was glad Mrs. Mellis left but she didn't show how she felt. She was good at that.

Unseen employees at several of the stores began rolling up the spider-web gates. Most of the other stores remain closed until 10 a.m. The few open shops were a couple of snack bars or a video arcade. Summer vacation was still several weeks away and then the little brats would be all over the place, she thought.

Maybe she would move to a warmer state, such as Arizona, she thought. Marilyn Harper moved to a retirement community just south of Tucson. She wrote how much she enjoyed it. The fresh desert air, the wide open spaces and barren mountains. The community catered to people her own age and offered such amenities like golf courses and tennis courts. However, the communities were probably overrun by the rats and she shuddered.

The woman stopped in front of the darkened travel agency. The posters of Hawaii and the Caribbean dotted the walls, but the one that caught her eye was a desert scene. The woman studied the poster. She noted what time the agency opened and continued on. She finished the four laps and rested a moment, then went out the double doors that led outside.

The spring day greeted her like a warm blast, the humidity rising with the temperature. Her bus had not arrived, so she waited in the shaded bus stop.

She refused to look at the young couple who slowly pushed a stroller past her. She couldn't see the crying infant buried beneath a pink blanket.

She thought back to when Frank was still alive. It seemed like yesterday when she pushed a stroller with Frank at her side. Now all that was gone leaving her alone with her memories.

Shaking her head to shoo the memories away, she stood up when the bus arrived. It was a little behind schedule, she noticed looking at her watch.

The End

NIGHT SWIM

It was a warm summer night and quite dark with few faint stars. What stars there were in the black night seemed to compete miserably with the glittering lights from the small harbor in the distance and the lights of the nearby town that spilled down like diamonds from the hills to the ocean.

The young couple sat on the blanket on the beach in front of a small fire. They could not see the waves, but they could hear the soothing, pounding sounds of the endless surf.

The young man stuck a marshmallow on the coat hanger and placed it over the fire watching it as it began to sizzle.

Cheryl did not say anything. She pulled the sweater over her bare legs tucked under her and wrapped her arms around herself.

"Let's go for a swim," he said.

"No. It's too cold."

"It's warm. You're crazy."

He took off his shirt as to prove it and picked up the coat hanger and turned it over and waited. He gently touched the marshmallow, but it was still hot. He waited until it cooled down and popped it in his mouth.

"Come on. The water is always warmer than the air at night."

"How do you know?"

"What do you mean how do I know? I've swam at night before."

"Oh, yeah? With who?" she said with a tone.

He didn't say anything and took his corduroy shorts off, still wet from the bathing suit underneath. "I'm going in," he announced and half ran down to the surf.

The water did indeed feel warmer, a reversal from the day when it felt cooler despite the hot sun. He went in to his knees and then looked back at the beach. He could see her, silhouetted by the fire, staring at the flames in deep thought. He turned and dove into the inky water. The white soup of the waves seemed to be phosphorus, like a million fire flies that ignited the water.

He opened his eyes under water, but of course he didn't see anything. He surfaced and saw a faint outline of a wave and swam for it. A strong swimmer, he rode the wave feeling the surge of the swell propel him forward. It was a weird sensation riding a wave at night.

All his other senses worked fine except his sight. He ducked out of the wave and came up and looked around. He swam on his back for about a hundred yards, then turned over and headed for shore. Something smacked into his leg, which startled him. He felt comfortable in the ocean, a good enough swimmer not to fear anything. He got out of the water and walked to the fire.

Cheryl, her head down eyes boring into the fire, did not acknowledge him. He wrapped a towel around himself and put on his sweater. He felt clean and happy, determined not to let her spoil the evening. "We need some more wood," he said, but she didn't respond. "I'll go get some."

He went to the pick-up and retrieved a couple of split medium size logs. Half way back he dropped one. "Damn it," he said and picked it up and placed it in the fire. The flames spat and crackled at him as if in anger.

"How's the water?" she said without feeling.

"Bitchin. You should of went in," he said, but she didn't answer.

"Do you want any more smores?" he asked.

"No. I'm full," she said.

He got a Grapheme cracker and stuck another marshmallow in the fire. When it was golden brown, he placed it between the crackers. It tasted good. Everything felt good, the cool sand on his feet, the salty feeling on his skin and in his hair, the warm glow of the fire and the smores. He glanced at the girl, whose attention seemed riveted on the glowing embers.

"Still in a bitchy mood?"

"So what," she hissed.

"It's a drag being around you sometimes."

"So don't," she threatened.

"I should have stayed in the water."

"Right."

"Something hit my leg. Maybe a shark," he teased, humming the theme song to the movie 'Jaws'.

"Uh uh."

She did not shift her gaze.

"Wanna go home?" he asked giving up. He could take her home, and then come back. He didn't know why he brought her. Maybe he would pick up Brandy and bring her back. Sometimes he got better company out of his golden retriever. He didn't have feelings anymore for the girl. He also believed she did not have feelings for him either.

"Let's go," he ordered, angry at her but not sure why.

She got up slowly and followed him obediently. She walked with her head down.

"Take me to Carlene's house."

"Yes, your highness."

"Don't..." she hissed, then in a calmer voice. "be a shit."

"Stick it," he said.

"You probably will after I'm gone."

He looked at her and shook his head.

"Just take me home," she said, getting into the car and slamming the door. "What about the fire?" she asked with suspicion.

"I'm coming back."

"With who?" she snapped.

"Maybe Brandy."

"A dog?" she said with a laugh. "That figures."

"She's much better company than you."

"Go to hell," she snapped.

He remembered a happier time when they laughed and talked and he felt comfortable with her. It was one of their first dates when they made love on the beach late one night almost at the same spot.

But things had changed in recent weeks. Her moods changed and she acted as if she was hiding something. Even her best friend acted differently around him as if she knew something.

He slammed on the brakes suddenly, almost throwing both of them against the dash board.

"Hey, you fucking bitch," he yelled with frustration. "I'm sick and tired of your stupid, bitchy comments. I'm sick of you... Get out. Now."

"What? Here?" she whined shocked by his outburst.

"Fuck you." He was angry and didn't want to blow up, but he did. He drove in silence angrily and a little too fast to her friend's house.

She said nothing, as she got out. She made sure she slammed the door again. He didn't care anymore. He went home to pick up his dog, which would be much better company anyway.

The End

DREAMS OF A CHILD

I awoke to a soft buzzing, a steady hum that penetrated my turmoil mind. It disappeared for a while, then came back and my eyes finally opened. I tried to focus on the bare room. I saw, before I actually felt, the fly land on my bare chest. I watched it for a moment until it flew away.

The rest of the adobe room came into focus gradually. I found myself in a barren, dusty room made of tired adobe walls, cracked and potted from centuries of use. The walls seemed in desperate need of repair. Holes in the adobe bricks allowed streams of sunlight to illuminate the dusty air.

The only furniture was a crudely made cot that I was lying on and an equally crude wooden chair that faced the cot. I studied the chair, then focused on what looked like the door. I failed to recognize it because of the dust and the haze.

I felt a sharp pain rocket to my head as I tried to get up. I flopped back down on the sweat-stained pillow made of straw. I clamped my eyes shut and grimaced until the pain subsided.

Drenched in a bath of sweat, I made another futile attempt to get up, but it was as if the pain was waiting for me. I tried to collect my thoughts and gather my strength.

I studied the mud thatch roof, which also needed repair. In one corner, the roof had caved in as if a giant fist had punched an opening. I figured that it was midday by the angle of the sun.

I wiped the sweat from my face with my left hand, while I tried to lift my right. I found I could not, which sent a shot of fear through my tormented mind. I managed to lift it and let out a breath of relief when I saw that I was not hurt. I didn't know why my hand felt so numb.

Once again I tried to get up and this time managed to swing my legs over the side of the cot. For the first time I felt the dirt floor. The pain slowly subsided, as I brushed my hair from my eyes with my good hand. I saw my white shirt on the edge of the cot and tried to put it on. I spent a few more moments gathering my strength.

I noticed my legs as if for the first time. I tried to stand and found it difficult. After standing for a moment, expecting any minute to fall, I started for the door.

Reaching it, I noticed that it was without a doorknob. Out of frustration I jammed my foot against it, surprised when it fell over into a dirt-strewn street. I found myself outside in a dusty plaza of an empty village with several other adobe buildings.

Squinting, my eyes slowly adjusted to the bright sunlight. I walked toward a dried-up stone fountain that sat stubbornly in the center of the square.

Ancient adobe buildings, just as old and worn out as the one I was in, surrounded the square on three sides. On the fourth side, a narrow, dusty road spilled out into the desert.

The hot steamy air felt dry and thick with dust and flies. A shot of pain ripped through my leg, causing me to buckle to the ground. Only my outstretch hands prevented a total collapse.

After a few moments of gathering my strength, I picked myself up from the ground. Using both hands and my right leg for leverage, I got to my feet and hopped the remaining way to the fountain. I sat down of the hot stone, nursing my leg, trying to find the source of the pain.

I scanned the buildings in hope of detecting any signs of life. I realized that I was totally alone. I decided to inspect each building in search for food and water.

I started with the two-story structure and headed for it. I peered into the open window into what was once an old hotel. I thought I saw some movement and called out to it. There was no reply.

I went around the side of the building in search for an entrance. Finally, I saw an opening and entered the hotel. A stream of sunlight from a window illuminated a table that sat against one of the walls.

As I drew nearer, I could see the table covered completely with ants. A ceramic plate crashed to the floor, which caused me to jump back.

I was about to leave, when I noticed a long, round, white object on the floor by the table. I would have gone to investigate it, but several ants had crawled up my leg causing great discomfort.

I glanced back at the object, illuminated by the sunlight, causing it to cast an eerie, ghostly glow. I went back to the building I awoke in and saw that the ants over ran the building like a successful army.

I went from one building to the next looking for help, but found no one. I retreated to the fountain and noticed a black swarm of ants covering the walls of the buildings.

It was at this moment, that I realized fear and confusion seeped into my body. I headed toward the opening of the village, where the plaza became the road. I headed out toward the desert.

I got to the edge where the town ended and the desert began. A moving swarm of ants covered the entire road for as far as I could see. Only the cactus and the Ocotillo bushes seemed to interrupt the flowing tide.

I retreated back to the plaza, humiliated by the fact that nothing more than mere ants forced me back. Ants that I would normally crush at will. I fought down my fears and studied the foe as it progressed toward the fountain from all sides.

The noise of the approaching army grew in intensity. The ground seemed to tremble. I felt a burning sensation and saw my right hand covered with ants. Covered so completely that I could not see the flesh. I shook my hand vigorously. Some of the ants fell off, but most clung to my skin.

Like a maniac, I started screaming at them to leave me alone, but they did not listen. I screamed of fear and panic, but they ignored that too.

I fell to the ground and the ants covered my face. I felt one beast crawl under my eyelid and I screamed in pain. All I could see was red. A loud painful red, only to be slowly replaced by black, a deep, impenetrable silent black.

****

I awoke to a soft buzzing and glared at the offender. Three red L.E.D.'s blinked the time at me. I tried to move my right hand, but realized that I had slept on it wrong. The numbing tingle in my hand slowly subsided.

The End

94

THE SALESMAN

The salesman pushed the lighted buzzer then stepped back and waited. Impatiently he pushed it again, this time without letting go until the door finally opened with a jolt. It opened slowly revealing an elderly lady who looked up at him with ancient brown eyes and a toothless grin.

The salesman was about to make his practiced speech when the woman beckoned him into a museum-like room by waving a gnarled hand at him. The reason that this was so shocking was that it was against the law for people to allow total strangers into their homes without written consent from the Office of Home security.

It was a long and difficult process in which first you had to swear that you trusted the stranger you wanted to invite into your home. Then you had to produce two witnesses, they had to be non-strangers, and put down a $1,200 fee. Three to four weeks later you got a card saying that you can allow only one person in.

If the person had a wife or friend, you had to pay an addition $500 per person or a $1,000 for anyone over a hundred and twenty years of age. That was the mandatory retirement age.

He was about to ask her if she had a card when she turned toward him and in a clear youthful voice that seemed to fit the woman somehow.

"Excuse me for letting you in. I know its forbidden but I'm very lonely and just had to have someone to talk to. I hope that I didn't trouble you too much."

She smiled sweetly at him and he was about to explain to her the law and its necessity.

"Why don't you go down to the Social Center where there are plenty of ol.. I mean.. people your age to talk to," he explained knowing that she wasn't listening to him. "It's not good sense to be seen talking to an Elder." He looked around suspiciously. He expected to see an agent jump out from under the couch or behind the door any minute. "I really should leave..." He stopped, noticing that the more he talked the wider her toothless grin became. He became disgusted with her and started to leave. Since the age of seven, they taught him, as all youths at that age are taught, the Forbiddens as well as going through the Studies.

For eight hours they place a student in a chamber where he is taught, with the help of a computer memory machine, the skills that in the old days took twelve years to complete. The computer sifted the mind for weakness and strengths and, more importantly, interests and focused on them. Then another four to six hours in the chamber produced a lawyer or engineer or a doctor.

The Forbiddens are a list of twelve hundred or so laws that are either strictly enforced or lenient enforced depending on the Director and his administration. The computer takes less than an hour to program the mind.

The Director currently in power is fairly lenient in interpreting the law. Especially in comparison to the last two Directors who ordered that singing was illegal and punishable by death. Now it was only a misdemeanor.

Now at the age of fourteen, the salesman has seen several Elders who tried to cling to the old way of life. A lifestyle that isn't totally banned except during the span of the last two directors. He would see them on his way home through the city. They would come up to people and ask for cigarettes or the time of day or directions even when they had all these things anyway.

Once an Elder came up to him and offered him a flower that was totally illegal and which made his eye's water and his nose about to tingle. He started to sneeze and didn't stop until they arrested the Elder and destroyed the flower.

He felt his eye's water and his nose tingled as he stood in front of the old woman. He began plucking his eye lids and opened the door to leave.

He left the old woman with the toothless grin and young voice and, with his eyes riveted on the ground in thought, went to the next house. He followed the cracks in the cement as they traveled helter skelter from one side of the sidewalk to the other.

He didn't see the power pole and he walked head on into it, knocking himself down. He was unhurt yet flushed with anger and embarrassment. He looked around to see if anyone saw him. He saw a man in the distance look at him, then quickly looked away. Except for that, he was certain no one saw him. He was unaware of the old woman who watched from her window, the idiotic grin still planted on her face.

He got up and brushed himself off and decided to try another neighborhood. He passed a few houses for good luck, before settling on a modern plastic home painted brown with an Astro turf lawn and green colored plastic plants surrounding the house. He was impressed with the plastic ivy that almost covered the high voltage barbwire fence, which separated the house with the one next to it.

He knocked on the synthetic wood door and waited patiently. He admired the plastic columns that pretended to support the porch when the door opened. He began his rehearsed speech in a singsong manner.

The middle-age woman opened the door with a sour look on her youthful face. She wringed her middle-age hands while she stared stupefied at the salesman. When he was through with his speech, he held out a sample of the product for her to look at. She looked at the product then back at the salesman before slamming the synthetic door in his face.

He felt relieved at this and began to walk down the steps past the fake lawn when he suddenly stopped to admire a row of plastic ducks. There was a large one followed by four smaller versions. Its black eyes straight ahead, its open beaks in silent honking.

He made his way back to the street satisfied at her attitude and that the Elders and their idiotic grins were few and far between. He was grateful that she didn't try to buy anything, didn't allow him into her home and didn't even speak to him.

They expected, even encouraged, this from the people, total suspicion of everyone. The art of door-to-door selling was almost extinct before the government revived it even the actual selling something was illegal.

He felt good about things seeing poker face residents peeking out of their barred windows like badly mutated rats. He was on the verge of a smile when he realized that someone might be watching him. Only when he left did they close their plastic curtains that covered iron bars.

The salesman returned to the office where he worked, his

briefcase bulging full of samples. He noticed his boss's door slightly open indicating that his boss was alone.

"I want you to close the deal... Yeah right.. Right... Sure. Damn it. Close it now. Well shit on them. Right fine." The boss slammed the phone down and stared at the salesman as if he was from another planet. He motioned for him to sit down.

"What do you have for me?" the boss asked gruffly.

The salesman opened the briefcase slowly and handed the reports over to the larger man. He scanned the pages rapidly, grunted then almost threw the report back to the startled salesman.

"You're doing fine kid. At this rate you'll make kiss ass man in no time."

The salesman beamed brightly at the prospect of becoming an assistant manager. He pulled his eyelids nervously, which disgusted his boss. Quickly dismissing the salesman with a sneer and a nod toward the door, the boss leaned back in his simulated leather chair and puffed on a synthetic Havana cigar. He praised the government for getting back Cuba and making it the 58th state.

The salesman went back to his own desk in the far corner of the room. Thirty keyboards were all going at once with an occasional cough or moan. There was no talking among the other salesman as they typed up their reports.

The salesman didn't notice the others. Whenever his mind went into a blank state, which usually happens when he lost himself in the stacks of papers, he was unaware of what was going around the office. He didn't even notice the blonde who leaned over him, her palms on the desk, her hair falling dangerously close to his face.

"How did you get that nasty bump on your head," she cooed. He finally noticed her when she put her long fingers on his bruised forehead.

"Ouch," he cried, leaning away from her.

"I sorry. Did I hurt you?" she whispered in her wine dark voice.

"Uh no." He waved at her fingers but missed.

"Are you afraid of me?" she asked with a laugh.

"Uh no," was all he managed to say. His throat was dry and parched as he swatted at her fingers again and missed again.

He found his eyes settling on her V-shape neckline that practically exposed her full reshaped breasts. A drop of perspiration fell on his waist beneath his shirt, which caused him to jump slightly. The blonde began to untie his tie with her ever-moving fingers.

"Uh don't," he muttered again leaning even further back in his chair. He could feel her breathe which smelled like a combination of chlorine and ammonia, which made him slightly noxious.

He got up, retrieving his tie from her fingers and slid by her and escaped to the men's room. Catching his breath, he turned the water on for no apparent reason except to drown the persistent tapping on the door. He looked around for a way to escape but found none. Out of shear boredom at looking at the blue urinals, he gave up and opened the door. The smiling blonde greeted him as she stood in front of the puffed-up face of his boss.

"What the hell are you doing in there?" the boss said, chewing on his cigar.

"Uh nothing," was all he could manage to say and he melted past them to his desk.

He sat looking at a picture of his mother who was represented on his desk by a three dimensional color photograph. It looked as if she was staring at him where ever he was.

The salesman lowered his eyes when the blonde walked by, her probing fingers dancing wildly in the air.

Only two more days until the weekend, he thought. He began thinking of things to do this weekend. He wanted to improve on last weekend. True, he did run the old lady over who was walking her poodle, then crashed his car into the gas pumps at the local station.

He was disappointed when he failed to cause the expected explosion. It did have its highlights when the station attendant ran buck naked through the gas as it spouted from the damaged pumps like a geyser. The attendant had a gas hose around his neck and laughing and screaming at the top of his voice.

The salesman wanted to join him, but was secured by the automatic seat belts. He did manage to bust out the window with his foot despite being all tangled up in the seat belt. The air bag, which suddenly inflated, smacked him in the face. He wanted this weekend to be better than last. He suddenly thought of the perfect weekend. His heart started to accelerate as the plan formed in his mind.

"That's it," he said out loud and getting up. He sensed twelve pairs of eyes on his including the blondes and he sat back down. Just two more days, he thought. He was unaware of the blonde as she leaned over again. She would be part of the weekend.

He ignored her, his thoughts elsewhere when the bell rang signifying the end of the shift. He began gathering his things as if to go home, knowing he didn't take anything home with him.

He tried to slide past the blonde when she grabbed him forcibly and pulled him onto his desk. He slowly realized that everyone else had disappeared leaving him all alone with her. He didn't think about calling for help as the blonde started ripping at his clothes. She began molesting him to the point of pain. He struggled with and noticed the door opening to his boss's office.

The blonde also noticed and released her grip a little, which gave the salesman time to slip away from her. He made it out the door just in time to avoid her and his boss.

When he got home, he took a shower to wash the nervousness from him but he couldn't stop shaking. He feared the blonde and felt ashamed by it. The next day he tried to avoid the blonde. He would make sure when it was time to go home they he wouldn't be left alone with her like the day before.

The next day after that was not much different either. He rarely saw the blonde as she left for lunch and did not to return.

He thought about telling someone, even thinking about going to the police and filing charges. He couldn't get the courage to go down to the station, since they would think that he was the one who started it. They would tell him that they had more important crimes to solve, giving examples such as the fugitive Amazon who murdered three men and was still at large. He realized that someone would have to kill him in order to get help.

He thought about the Elder woman who invited him into her house the other day. He thought of her smooth youthful skin and her idiotic grin and her gnarled hand reaching out to him.

The salesman decided to endure the humility of the abuse himself. He only had to wait until next year, when the Office of Human Development would fix him up with someone to mate, someone that was his exact specification.

This was known to eliminate divorce and allowed the burden of courtship to fall on the government and not on the individual. This eliminated broken engagements and murder from jealous rivals and love because it would obsolete caring.

If in the rare case that two people didn't get along and the computer was unusually wrong, one of the couples had an option of suicide. If neither took that option, then they would be executed together.

The salesman thought of himself as unfit for marriage and future membership into the Society. He thought about going to the island of Ylek Reb, a former Russian island off the coast of Nevada where Elders, Perverts, Homos, unmarried and other exotic people lived.

The small island is all that remains of the states of Washington, Oregon and California, which Russia invaded and took over after the big quake of '22 that hit the west coast.

The office was beginning to empty for the weekend. At first he panicked at the thought of being left alone with the blonde, but then remembered she had left at lunch. Still he did not want to be left alone, so he hurried to catch up with his co-workers.

The walk home was exciting to him in anticipation for the weekend, which started at six tonight and lasted till 6 Sunday night.

When he got to the door he was shocked to see it jimmied open. Something told him not to go in but he found himself pushing the door open. His apartment was in shambles, but before he could utter a cry, a hand grabbed him from behind.

One sweaty hand covered his mouth, while a powerful hairy arm wrapped itself around him and forced him to the floor. He could feel the noxious breath on his neck. Just then the attacker relented his control and stood up panting. The salesman turned, shocked to see that it was his boss.

"What are you doing here?" the salesman replied weakly. His lower lip trembled as he tried not to show fear.

"I didn't know who you were," his boss said coarsely. He waved at the ramshackle room.

"I didn't do this. I got here a few minutes before you did and found it like this." His boss looked at the salesman for a few nervous seconds.

"Does anyone have any reason to do this to you?" his boss asked.

The salesman just shook his head and pulled on his eyelids. His boss looked at him pitifully and stalked out the door in hopelessness.

"Lock the door behind me," he warned without looking back.

The salesman obeyed him, then turned to face the room. Surveying the room, he heaved a sigh and headed for the bathroom. He was determined to soak away his fears with a hot bath. He turned on the lights to the rest room and noticed someone was already in the blue tile tub. He backed up and started to apologize when he realized that it was his own place. He was not surprised to see the blonde sitting diligently in the soapy water.

She looked up at him and smiled seductively. For several seconds they stared at each other, before the blonde stood up, unconcerned with her nakedness. She giggled at an apparent thought and the salesman blushed profoundly, his eyes growing wider. She grabbed a towel and walked past him, while the salesman tugged on his eyelids.

She looked around the living room, then said proudly that she didn't mean to wreak his place and she didn't have much time and produce what she was after.

"Just what are you after?" he asked, wondering since she was standing there with a towel around her waist.

"You know and I won't leave until I get it," her voice was suddenly harsher and colder.

"I honestly don't know what you are looking for," he stammered. He didn't sound anything like the confident salesman. He began to whimper.

"Oh, stop it you silly pig," she spat.

"You know damn well what I'm looking for and I intend to get it. With or without your help. She took his arm and twisted it so he had to fall to his knees.

"I won't," he cried in agony. "I won't. Damn you. You know I'll never give it up."

It felt as if she was twisting his arm off.

"Get up you fool. Get up," she screamed, then out of frustration she went outside.

When he was sure she had left he went to his bedroom and with a pocket knife turned his mattress over and ripped the bottom of the mattress apart. He smiled broadly carefully wrapping the small wooden box in an article of clothing. He stuffed the bundle under his arm and locked himself in the bathroom. He ran the water in the sink then rechecked the door to make sure it was locked.

He sniffed the aromatic box, reveling in the deep smell of real cherry. With nervous fingers he toyed with the ancient latch. The box was no more than twelve inches long and six inches deep by four inches wide. The contents were far more important for such a small box, even for this rare wood.

He was overwhelmed at being assigned this task to safeguard the box. He couldn't say no to his government. They didn't tell him that the enemies of the government would stop at nothing to get what was in the box.

With courage, he opened the box and stared at the contents with awe. Except for a few of the Elders he was one of a few people who had seen the contents. Feeling his hand's sake, he put the box down on the sink.

A sudden pounding on the front door startled him and he began to panic. The pounding was followed by a vicious crash and he knew that they were inside his flat. Almost immediately the pounding was on the bathroom door and he knew he had little time. He looked around for a place to hide it but he knew they would find it in a short time.

He remembered the Director's orders once again in his mind, telling him the enemies must not get its hands on the box. He always thought of himself as the best agent the Director had.

The door was almost off the hinges and in a few seconds, they would be inside. He had to act fast. He grabbed the contents and put them in his mouth. The taste was bitter and he screwed his face up in protest. Before they grabbed him and tried to get him to cough it up he had swallowed them completely.

"Damn it," screamed his boss, pounding his fist on the sink, almost cracking the plastic counter. His puffy red face worked feverishly on a cigar. The salesman saw the worry in his face.

"Damn it," the blonde screamed, still wearing only the towel.

She slugged the large mirror above the sink sending glass everywhere.

Seeing that they could do nothing about it, the blonde and her boss and several other large men, who the salesman never seen before, all retreated out the bathroom.

They left the salesman not really knowing what he swallowed. Of course he read about it and knew its importance, but didn't know what they were for.

As he drained the soapy, scummy water from the tub he said the word over and over in his mind. It sounded important enough, as he rubbed his throat.

The End

LOOKING BACKWARDS

He awoke in a bath of sweat, adjusting his eyes from the brightness of the dream to the darkness of the room. He felt the body next to him. It was warm and soft and he could not remember who it was.

"What were you laughing about?" asked the sleepy voice under the covers.

"Nothing."

"What?"

"Nothing," he said louder.

The figure sat up next to him but said nothing. She was naked, except for the sheets that cover her legs.

"Thanks for waking me. Now that's two things you're good at."

"What's that supposed to mean?"

"Jesus," she sighed and flopped back on the pillow. "Men are really stupid sometimes," she announced.

"Fuck you bitch," he said, not really angry.

"Shit yes, we're bitches when we have such ass's chasing our asses," she said bitterly.

"That's real nice."

"Isn't it?"

"Shut up," he whispered, more to himself.

"Make me."

There was a long silence that he could not take. It had been good in the beginning. The times at the beach, the dinners at their favorite restaurant. For some reason it turned ugly. They no longer talked. They no longer cared. He got out of bed wishing he was somewhere else.

"Shit," he cursed and left the room.

He knew that she would not follow him. He went to the kitchen and took out a beer and twisted the cap off. He took a couple of gulps needing to relax.

****

The dream seemed so real. He was in a room without walls. He lay on what seemed like a white, marble floor. A floor that seemed to illuminate by itself. He saw no ceiling or walls and he did not hear a sound. He tried to sit up, succeeding on the second try. The luminous floor seemed to stretch to infinity. He got to his feet slowly, only then noticing that he had on a dark, navy-blue T-shirt and fog-gray shorts. He was barefoot, but the floor did not feel cold.

"This has got to be a dream," he said more to himself than to anyone in particular.

The answer startled him. He whirled around to face the man. Not an old man but not a young man either. A powerful man who looked vulnerable. He wore a beard and his hair was wavy. Nick stepped backwards.

"Who are you?" he asked, but the bearded man didn't answer right away.

He walked around Nick as if inspecting him.

"Do you know why you are here?" the bearded man asked in a voice as dry as a desert wind.

"This some kind of health club?" Nick said, scanning the room. "Or the funny farm."

"I don't understand."

"Read my lips, Moses," Nick said suddenly afraid. "Who the hell are you and where the hell is this?"

"That's a possibility," the bearded man said in humor, but no smile was evident.

"What's that supposed to mean?" Nick asked, but the other didn't answer.

He turned as if to face an audience, his arms extended as if he was walking a tight rope.

"What troubles you the most?" the bearded man asked.

"Say again?"

"In life. Where do you find the most pain? The most concern?" the bearded man asked.

"You talk funny."

"Is that your answer?" the other said with a glance.

Nick thought for a moment pawing at the floor with his bare foot.

"Jobs," he summarized as if asking himself.

"Truly?"

"Chicks. I suppose. A job doesn't give me as much grief as a chick would. Well, maybe you do know. You married?"

"Why should poultry bother you?"

"Poultry?"

"You said chicks bother you."

"Chicks, broads, girls," Nick said, as if he was talking to himself. "Yooo Hoo. What planet are you from? I didn't realize there were any hippies left. I like your ideas of sex and dope though."

"What if you were given the opportunity to face your problems face to face," the bearded man said, facing Nick now.

"What do you mean?"

"What if you could face a room full of women? Women who you have known from your past. Friends, lovers, girlfriends. What would you say to them?"

"I would tell them all to take a flying leap."

"I detect anger and bitterness within your soul," the bearded man said.

"You detected right, old holy one. I also detected a lot of weirdness with your get up and this glowing floor. That's all there seems to be around here is this floor and you."

"What else do you want?"

"My room back and that chick I was banging. A bitch to the max, but what a great ass," Nick smiled.

"Are you truly happy with this woman?"

Nick thought it over before answering.

"No."

"Are you happy with this physical relationship?"

"No, I guess not," Nick said, turning away from the man. "For a dream, this is sure a weird one. So what's the answer, hippie man?"

"Face your past," came the answer.

When Nick turned around, the man had disappeared. He spun around again and he was facing his past. There they all were, just sitting there. Sitting on a bright, pure-white marble seats. He couldn't believe his eyes. Carol with her sweet country smile. She was not pretty, but she had a goodness that made her more attractive.

Next to her was Loretta. Bright, funny, beautiful Loretta. She was like an angel, challenging the floor for brightness honors. She looked at him with a look of regret.

And Sally. A good friend who stuck by him for years even when she moved away. She always wrote him or called him. Always caring. She married and had several kids, but she was always there. She looked older, but still the same somehow.

And Kammy. She was young and pretty, but with little ambition in life except to party and tease men. She teased him beyond control but he didn't mind. Others were there too. Some he forgot their names. They were all women he had known at one time. Women he had dated, loved, fought and cared for and thought about.

"Jesus shit," he breathed, taking a step backwards. He looked around for the bearded man, but he found himself alone with his problem. There was no place to hide.

"Face your problem," a voice said behind him. He turned and saw the bearded man standing right behind him.

"Are they real?" Nick asked.

"Of course."

"But how? I mean how did you know who they were? I don't even remember some of them."

"Does it matter?"

"How did they get here?" Nick asked. "They lived in four or five different states."

The other didn't speak and Nick turned and faced the group.

"Why?" Was all he could think of.

"Why what?" Someone spoke.

"Just why? Why the excuses? Why the lies? Why the misunderstandings and why the hatred. Why didn't it ever work out? Was it me?" He stopped unsure of the direction he was going.

"Maybe you tried too hard," Sally said, who always tried to have an answer. She always seemed to care the most.

"Maybe I was just trying, period. Next time I'll just beat the shit out of you and treat you like shit. Women seem to like that."

He turned his back to them and faced the bearded man.

"Okay gramps. Snap your fingers and send me back to Kansas."

"There's one more young lady you should face," the old/young man said.

"Who?" Nick asked turning around. "Her? No way. I'm not a cradle robber. Even when I was thirteen, I always chased older..." he stopped and turned back to the man.

"She's your daughter," the other explained.

"My what? That can't be. I don't have... Who?" He turned back to the problem again. He looked at the one he guessed would be the mother.

"Kristie?" he whispered.

She nodded, looking at him with emotion.

"Why didn't you tell me?" He glanced at the girl. She was about eight, pretty and so small among the others. "Why the hell didn't you tell me."

She shook her head, tears welling up in her eyes. "I'm sorry." Was all she could say.

"Yeah right. Get me out of here." He turned again.

"Not yet," the other said in anger.

Nick glared at him, but said nothing.

"Nice guys finish last. Is that it?" Nick said to no one in particular or maybe to everyone.

"That's not it," Loretta said. Beautiful, intelligent Loretta.

"Then what is it?" he yelled, startling even himself.

"I can't speak for anyone but myself. I just didn't want to get serious with anyone. I told you that," she said.

"Then why did you avoid me?"

"Because I didn't want to lead you on."

"Maybe you didn't want to lead yourself on?" He always wanted to say that.

She looked stunned, but didn't answer.

A girl stood up in back. He couldn't place her name, but her face was familiar.

"And you are?" he said sarcastically.

"Carol," she said shyly.

"Kinda rings a bell," he said, not really remembering.

"I didn't think you would remember," she said as if he was going to hit her.

"I remember. I'm surprised your here."

"Why?"

"Cause I thought this was the chicks.. I mean women I cared about," he said folding his arms on his chest.

Carol shook her head.

"No?"

"No. You see the tables can be turned," she said.

Nick didn't say anything to that.

"What about me? What about my feelings?" she whispered.

"What about.. I mean. I know. I know. Turn around is fair play. So it stinks doesn't it."

"I know," she said, sitting down as if to make her point.

"Where is my bearded friend," Nick said, turning around again. He stared at the floor in silence.

"It wasn't all your fault," a voice said. "We are to blame too. Then maybe it was no one's fault."

"Love stinks. Like that song says."

"It isn't fair for all of us. Not just you," someone said. It was Loretta.

"So what happens now?" he asked wanting her. Of all the woman in his life, she was the one who moved him the most. He turned again to face her.

She sat in the front row, staring at him with those deadly blue eyes. 'Go away' His mind screamed at her, at all of them, but his heart and loins wanted them all. He pounded the floor with his fist in frustration.

"Stop it. Make them go away," he said and suddenly it went dark and they did.

He woke in the night in a bath of sweat. He felt the body next to him. It was warm and soft.

"What were you laughing about?" the sleeping voice asked from under the covers.

"Nothing," he said confused. Was I laughing? "Nothing," he repeated for no reason.

The End

THE ALLEY

The walls of the cold, concrete canyon towered over the figure as it slithered its way down the narrow alleyway. The form stopped when it emerged into the entrance of an empty street.

It stood, half in the darkness that oozed out from the alley and half in the street light that threatened to reveal its identity. Looking from a distance like a crazed monk, the shadow bowed to an unseen temple, then straightened up and with a quick look around evaporated back into the darkness from which it came. What it left behind, went mostly unnoticed to the few that still wandered aimlessly through the night.

It wasn't until four hours later when a bag lady pushing a wire-frame grocery cart stopped and bent over to examine the object with hopes to salvage it. She peeled away the rags slowly then when she realized what it was, started screaming hysterically, attracting a small crowd of fellow night people.

The object, somehow on its own power, rolled from a bloody pool that formed beneath it, off the sidewalk and into the street where it came to a rest. It's pale bluish white skin, eerie in the dim street light. Its eyes were wide in amazement and its bloody mouth formed what seemed to be a knowing grin.

****

The clear greenish water erupted out from the top of the stone fountain only to fall back into the circular pool that surrounded the granite volcano. Scores of tarnished pennies and dimes littered the blue-green mosaic tile bottom.

Dave watched without much interest as the fountains ominous spray made ever-changing patterns as it fell back into the pool. He

glanced briefly at the throngs of people walking in every direction
through the indoor arcade of the mall. His dark, blue eyes studied
the shoppers, especially a pretty blonde who slowly made her way
past the various windows with its many items on display.

Rows and rows of clothing were lined up like soldiers in a never
ending march to battle, signs and ads pleading this sale or that
bargain. Her wary eye scanned the items with professional
keenness. She also watched the people pass around her like
dodging running backs in an insane football game.

Finally, she sensed a pair of eyes on her and she turned around
toward Dave who glared back at her from across the mall. She
smiled shyly but when he continued his cold hard gaze, her own
smile vanished and mistrust and suspicion seeped in. The speck of
doubt marred her outlook and irritated her, her face darkening
momentarily like a threatening storm. Like all storms, her
expression passed and she resumed an air of calm, glancing back at
the window display. Her pace quickened with a hint of anxiety. She
knew from experience the intentions of most people, especially
men, whether friendly or not.

What gave her a feeling of discomfort was his empty gaze that
seemed to penetrate her soul. Her attention shifted to a display in
the clothing store and her lithe form disappeared into the store.

Dave continued to stare at the entrance to where she
disappeared. His mind raced through a kaleidoscope of emotions,
finally stopping on hatred. Not really hatred at her, but hatred at
his own inabilities. He found himself staring down at the base of
the fountain in a darker mood than before. His emotions traced the
Spanish mosaic tile.

"Damn," he said out loud, loud enough that a middle age woman
sitting nearby glance over in bewilderment.

"What am I, invisible?" he asked, then laughed in sarcasm at his
own rebuke.

The woman, her handsome face brown and lean, looked up from
her book and eyed him coldly. She rose from the semi-circular
stone bench and quickly gathered her belongings and left.

Dave did not notice that she had left, since he was noticing
himself under his dark blue wind breaker. It hid his slender features
but at least he could see himself. He pawed the ground with his
sneaker, and then pounded his fist down of the bench, not hard
but just as forceful. He did not look up, but he sensed several pairs

of eyes on him. He stood up and headed to the escalators that carried shoppers to the second level.

He had no particular destination. He just had to keep moving so as not to dwell on one subject. It was always the case when he sat in one spot, his mind would ponder, stare, analyze and evaluate something or someone, someplace, repeatedly until his emotions would rise and he would have to move again. Being on the move was a needed change that seemed to calm him and assure him. He walked with a half concealed limp. Not that there was anything wrong with his leg. It was just a way to draw attention or sympathy to himself. Most people simply ignored him. But a few would eye him with nothing more than a curious glance.

A salesgirl stood behind a counter with a bored expression painted on her made-up strained face. Her face caked with mascara and eye shadow. An obese woman, her hands full of packages, trailed by three small children. An elderly man leaning on a knarled walnut cane thinking of long ago memories of youth.

All used Dave as a brief escape from their monotonous thoughts. He felt silly for faking the limp but when he thought about it he realized that it could prove useful.

"Hey kid," an ominous voice came from a direction. Dave glanced around. "Hey punk. Up here. Yooo Hooo," the voice bellowed again, more harsher, drawing stares.

Dave spun around in confusion then finally looking up into the hard, weather-beaten bearded face of his uncle who was hanging over the railing of the second story.

Dave welcomed the intrusion on his thoughts as well as the break with the loneliness. His uncle was a combination of a comical buffoon, the village idiot and the biggest pain the ass one can be associated with. He felt a sense of comfort though when he was in his presence despite the patience ending frustration that usually resulted after a prolong encounter. The reason he felt comfortable was probably due to the opposite personalities. One a middle age, free spirited obnoxious Irishman with a careless attitude and the other, an angry somber, deeply intense troubled young man.

"Davy. You son of a bitch. Where the hell have you been?" his uncle bellowed unconcerned, with the stares. "I have been looking all over this over-grown grocery store looking for you," the older man said. "You said to meet me by the bookstore at noon and it's almost one."

Dave looked at him coldly, not remembering any planned meeting.

"Oh shit. Doesn't matter. I forgive you this time. Been chatting with this good looking broad over in Sears. Man she had the nicest pair of... Dave, are you listening?"

"The escalator is over there," Dave said, trying not to raise his voice. "Come down so we don't have to shout."

"What?" the older man said with a smile. Dave looked up at him oddly, before motioning for him to descend.

While waiting for his uncle he found himself staring at three nuns who were making their way slowly through the flowing mass. They stopped on occasion to study the various shops or to marvel at the vastness of the mall. He had always been afraid of nuns. He did not know why and he thought that it was silly. Maybe it was the aura about them. He found it hard to accept that they were ordinary sensitive women.

The nuns disappeared into a store when his uncle sauntered up, grinning from ear to ear like a sailor back from leave.

"Anyway. What I was saying about this broad. The one is Sears with the huge hooters. She was yakking about some friend of hers who..."

Dave was only half listening, trying hard not to, and in danger of falling into autistic distortion.

"It's funny how chicks spill their life story out to total strangers. Anyway this kids of hers..."

Dave's thoughts drifted on, over and over, his mind filtering for a topic to settle on, straining the used thoughts that sifted through his mind in cycles. Finally, a concept was planted, only to wait and be carefully cultivated. The ominous presence of his uncles constant babbling temporarily interrupted the flowering thought.

"Man alive. You never saw anything so funny in your life. Imagine..."

There. Finally. The seed was planted and the outside interruptions removed and he finally drifted away, his thoughts taking shape and form. The images were clear now, like a movie ready to be viewed for the first time. The first few frames were in remembrance of past romantic encounters which were not that many and not that romantic.

Sure he went out with girls in the past, even slept with a few, but there was nothing special. No fireworks, nothing to write home about. The thought of a permanent relationship scared him as much as a lack of one depressed him. He could not picture himself with a wife who was gradually losing her looks and her personality.

Spending more and more time in front of the soaps or reading the trash magazines. Their two creepy kids in constant screaming tantrums. No thanks, he thought. He felt relieved that he wasn't in that situation. He knew a few people who were. Yet he couldn't cope with the ominous presence of being single and alone either.

The television ads depicting the cute, clean couple, jogging or eating cereal with their cute quiet children. He couldn't read a magazine or a newspaper without seeing society's obsession with dating, sex and affairs. It seemed that everyone gawked at single people as if there was something wrong with you.

Suddenly he realized that something was wrong. There was silence. He turned to see that his uncle was staring at him. Finally, in a voice as serious as he ever heard his uncle use.

"What's eating you boy?" his uncle asked. "I know that once I start babbling it's easy to head for dreamland but you have a strange look on your face. What's wrong?"

"Nothing," Dave said with slight annoyance, alerted to the seriousness of the other's tone. "Nothing's wrong. Just thinking about paying rent."

"Bullshit. Don't give that. You know me or your mom would help you out any time." Then in a softer voice.

"What's the problem boy?"

Dave stared at his uncle, trying to read the intent of his expression. Was he serious in helping or would he just tell his mother.

"Women. My life really. It's uh… not going anywhere. I can't explain it. I work at a crummy job picking leaves off of a lousy sidewalk and cleaning barbecue grills. Most guys my age are out of school with a degree, working with computers and joining country clubs, belonging to..." He stopped, unsure of what he was trying to say.

"Belonging to someone. Me? I have no one," he shrugged, his shoulders as if to emphasize his distress.

"A lot of guys are stuck in high stress jobs they hate with nagging boring wives and snotty nose brats," his uncle said. "They would love to trade places with you."

"I know, I know," Dave said. Somehow it sounded different

when someone else said it.

"There are a lot of guys worse off than you too. Drug addicts who can't take a shit without a fix or those so-call party animals who brag about the wonderful time they are having. But are they?"

"They sure act like it."

"Acting man," his uncle said, with a sly grin. "Facades. They are expert at hiding how they really feel. You're not the only one with problems. Everyone does. Except of course me."

Dave studied the serious-silly face of the older man. His confused mind refused to come up with a retort. Especially since he knew his uncle was right.

"You can only be as happy as you want to be," his uncle paused to let that sink in. "No one has the power to make you happy or sad. We all base our hopes on someone else or a religion or some new fad but it's really ourselves that we have to rely on. You have to stand up and know where you want to go. That doesn't mean to build yourself up to someone you are not. There's a line between confidence and egotism. Between confidence and the lack of it."

He saw a different expression on his nephew's face. Not one of confusion or anger or rage but one of enlightenment. He smiled and slapped the younger man on the back. They walked out of the mall and into the parking lot. The air was warm and fresh.

Dave felt a temporary, satisfying feeling invade the coldness and hatred of his mind.

****

The young woman peered into the half opened refrigerator sifting through the various assortments of bottles and jars. With a frown she selected an odd shape bottle from the back.

She somehow managed to maneuver it out from the maze of jars only to drop it onto the floor spilling the multicolor gelatin capsules everywhere. She sighed, shrugging her thin shoulders in defeat as if she knew all along that this was going to happen.

She began the task of picking up as many of the capsules as she could and funneling them back into the jar. She stared at the remaining few that lay on the floor. With a shrug, she swept the pills under the frig except for two that she swallowed without water. She put the jar back next to another jar with a greenish liquid that looked like melted Jell-O.

She surveyed the rest of the bottles. Ignoring a few old wrinkled carrots, passing over the remains of a brown stained lettuce, which rapidly turned black and started to smell. She scanned the bottles again. They contained every possible juice, carrot, celery, lettuce, even pomegranate juice. There was also every kind of vitamin and mineral tablets.

She stood undecided between wheat germ and GORP, which was a mixture of everything and anything. The girl-woman, depending on one's definition of a mature child or an immature woman, shook her sandy color hair in frustration. She closed the grime-covered door and flowed slowly back to her simple, untidy living room, which dominated her simple, untidy apartment.

Something out of the corner of her eye caught her attention. Upon investigation she found that she had left her iron face down on her blouse. It was rapidly turning from a dingy white to a charred brown. She let out a cry of desperation that caused a dog of unknown breeding to look up with a start. The dog then began attacking its own hind leg violently.

The girl, dressed in an over-size T-shirt and faded blue jeans, sat down hard on a dusty couch. The dog joined her as it bounded happily onto her lap. She, in frustration or anger or both, pushed the animal away and stomped from the room like a spoiled child throwing a tantrum.

Decided she needed a shower, she entered the small cluttered bathroom and began to undress. An army of bluish pimples covered her small, but firm breasts. She had a thin waist and thighs that she thought still weren't thin enough. Her sturdy legs and bony knees were supported by pencil thin ankles.

The water, already a half foot deep in the tub due to a clogged drain, went from semi-hot to luke warm and finally cold almost immediately which promptly signaled the end of the shower.

She got out of the stall with shampoo still in her hair and went in search for a towel. Finding none, she stopped in front of the mirror, dripping on the bare floor unsure of what to do.

After a while she climbed back into her jeans and shirt. Leaving a trail of water, she went back to the living room and sat down on the couch and began to comb her hair, shaking it occasionally to dry it. She waited for the phone call which in the back of her mind would not come. The dog, sat on the sand covered couch and stared at her with a hurt expression. It did not advance toward the human unless it got some sort of affection or sympathy.

The girl laid her head back, feeling the warmth of the sun filtering through the partially opened blinds. The sun felt good on her face as she let her thoughts drift among the salty sea air. Startled she opened her eyes and looked around in confusion. She saw the dog lying on the floor, its thin belly rising and falling with every difficult breath. She eyed the quiet phone and looked at the digital clock that told her that it was four hours later. She did not hear the knocking on the door until she heard the voice calling out her name.

"Darlene. It's me, Maggie." Silence filled the room, then the rapping on the door growing louder as did the impatient voice.

"Darlene," the voice said. "Are you awake. Are you okay. Of course you're okay," the voice answered itself.

The dog woke suddenly and began to bark. The woman woke in a stupor and opened the door for her friend.

"Oh. Hi Mag. I must have dozed off," Darlene said, looking at the phone. "That jerk didn't call last night," she pouted.

Maggie pretended not to hear. She leaned over and patted the dog on the neck giving it momentary pleasure. It pulled away from the girl's hand and jumped on the couch.

"I think I saw him at morning service with some girl. The one who's old man owns the apartments on Third Street," Maggie said.

"He what?" the thin girl gasped. Maggie didn't answer. She stared at the dumbness of the dog that fell asleep again. An uncomfortable silence prevailed over the two friends as Maggie scanned the unkempt apartment. She looked at her friend who stared at the floor, her eyes welling up. She looked up at her friend, secretly jealous of the other girls looks.

She remembered when they met in a self-defense class given at the local junior college. They sat next to each other and soon became partners. They slipped into a guarded conversation and finally into a guarded friendship. They had fun times together but they lacked the close comfortable feeling.

"Well screw him," Darlene said breaking the silence. "Who needs him," she added.

"Right," the other agreed. "I have to leave. I just stopped by to see how you were doing," Maggie said with a smile.

"Okay."

"I'll see you later?" A guilty wave swept over her and she added without considering.

"How about coming over Tuesday night," she remembered that she was busy and she was about to reverse her plans.

"I have a tie-dye class on Tuesday," Darlene said and Maggie heaved a sigh yet pretended disappointment.

She was out the door saying that they should get together sometime. Darlene hardly was aware that she left. She shut the door catching the dog who was half way outside.

****

The figure sliced its way through the pre-dawn night, invisible except when passing a lighted area and then only long enough to leave a cold shadow faintly on the gray concrete wall. Where it was headed was unknown to any observer. Only the figure knew of its destination due to the anxiety shown in the way it tilted its head and the swiftness of its stride.

The figure came to the edge of a well-lighted and well-traveled street. At this hour though, there was few pedestrians still wandering around without aim, in search of purpose or hope. Persistent drunks or insomniacs or suicidal depressants, all looking ragged, most of them old, all forlorn. Perennial loners who clung to city sidewalks for protection against the fears and horrors that surrounded them.

The figure observed them with ardent hatred. He scanned the people around him, revealing a sliver of his face, the face of a young, distressed man with cold hatred burning within him. His eyes were like coals that glowed brightly in the darkness. His mind raced in random, finally letting his instincts guide him. He found himself staring at a solitary drunk whose unsteady path seemed to head straight for the figure.

The figure froze momentarily, a gasp stranded in his throat. He finally exhaled in silence as the derelict without looking up, ambled close by. When he passed, his back to the dark image, the young man moved quickly almost too quickly, upon him.

Before he reached him, the old man turned around suddenly with unusual speed, which caused the younger man to stop momentary, unsure of what to do.

"Ohhh," the old man cried, but then relief came to his broken, elderly face with bright, blue eyes, not unlike his grandfather.

"I couldn't sleep sir. I thought I would go for a walk. To unwind," the drunk said, with a strong Eastern Europe accent. He smiled up at the younger man and pointed a wrinkled finger at his head as if to show what he meant.

The figure waited, his anger rising from within, anger and frustration at the drunk and all drunks. He was angry at their loneliness or his. At their defeatist attitude or his. Angry at the old man and himself. Restraining his rage for a moment he guided the old man into the safety of the darkness. Safe because he could not see the sad face looking up at him.

The dark figure pulled a heavy bar from his pea coat and with a groan brought it down on the old man's head, cracking it like a cantaloupe and spilling its contents on the sidewalk. The young man, without expression except in the eyes, wiped off the bar with the old man's beer soaked coat.

He looked around then vanished into the alley, to be swallowed into the night, leaving only the sound of a distant siren fading slowly in the distance.

****

He awoke from the nightmare with a lurch, his face covered with sweat. It took him a few minutes to familiarize himself with his surroundings before he could calm himself down. He vaguely remembered what the dream was about. Someone or something was hunting him, chasing him but he never saw who it was. They were similar to other dreams.

In this dream he was on a familiar street waiting for someone to emerge from one of the abandon buildings when all the sudden, a dull numbing pain shot through him. A pain like that of a knife being thrusted into his back. It was a bone numbing pain that remained even when he woke.

He looked down to discover the alarm clock that normally sat on the night table, was now on the bed. He must have knocked it over and rolled over it. He laughed to himself relieved that it was only a dream, yet mystified by the closeness of the reality to dreams. He replaced the clock then dropped his head back down on the pillow, his eyes closed.

A faint cry from a passing freight train beckoned him, seducing him with promises of adventures and escape. The moment simply vanished, the train swallowed up by the orchestra of crickets and an occasional passing car.

****

The old Buick made its way into the apartment complex parking lot. It was early morning, the sky, gray and heavy with a threat of rain. Dave got out and made his way through the carefully manicured Japanese gardens to the rental office where Mr. Grambell waited for him. He was a short roly-poly man with a shiny bald pate and a fat puffy face. He would always be drinking a cup of coffee or smoke a cigar, which hung from his lips.

Mr. Grambell greeted him when he arrived. Not friendly, yet not altogether unfriendly either. He would try some small talk, but with either the differences in ages or Dave's cold personality, he would give up. He disappeared into the back office, dabbing at the perspiration on his forehead. He came back out moments later, turning off the lights and locking the door.

"Let's make the rounds," he would say stopping to study the tinted glass windows.

"And the windows could use some work," he would sometimes say too. The rounds would turn out to be a tenement parking lot that circled the complex like a moat.

Dave's job was to police the lot in an electric golf cart. It was dull and the periodical chatter of his boss, who always drove the stupid cart, bored him. When they finished, he would drop Dave off at the tool shed where all the supplies were kept.

He would give him simple directions to clean the laundry room, the recreation room near the pool, the bathrooms and the barbecue grills that were placed throughout out the complex. Occasionally he would allow him to fix up an apartment after a tenant moved out. This provided slight relief from the tedium.

Every other morning an elderly tenant in his eighties would lecture him about something that was wrong with the apartment. The old man had nothing better to do than bellow at innocent victims, usually the young. This particularly morning, he cornered Dave and began flailing his skinny arms like a pale windmill.

Dave would let him run his coarse, then smile and walk away in vain. The old man, in victory would waddle back to his darken apartment, continuing the argument over his shoulder.

As Dave headed back to the office he glanced up at the window of an upstairs apartment. The curtains were drawn now, but he would be back later to catch a glimpse of her.

When he got back to the office, the manager gave him a slip that had an apartment number on it and a complaint. He saw the complaint and the number and grimaced, then headed off in the general direction.

When he arrived at the door, he wasn't surprised to see the door already open and a middle age woman with flaming red hair, standing there. She had a face saturated with freckles that might have been pretty long ago. Without a word, she beckoned him into a crowded living room.

A cat, trailed by three smaller balls of fur and legs, walked around as it owned the place. It neither noticed the woman nor the stranger. It passed under a covered bird gage without paying attention to that either. A chirping came from the cage, then stopped when the threat was gone.

Dave looked politely at the usual pictures that rimmed the hutch. One picture looked familiar, then he realized it was the woman as a young girl. The woman who had left the room came back in.

"It's in here," she said, barely above a whisper. She pointed to the room that she had just come from.

He slowly entered what he guessed a bedroom because of an old mattress that sat in the corner. He was surprised to see the room this way since the rest of the apartment was immaculate. There were scraps of newspaper and rags and pieces of carpet.

The woman pointed to the corner of the room and Dave saw why she summoned him. In the corner was the carcass of a small animal. It smelled bad and began to draw ants. He wrapped the carcass in some rags and newspapers and took it outside into fresh air in search for the dumpster. He didn't see the dripping blood until he got outside.

"Don't forget the ants," the woman said with a smile.

"I'll have to get the spray from the shed," he said, coming back. He wiped his hands on the rags but they still smelled. She nodded and folded her arms and stood in the doorway as is telling him to hurry.

****

The boy, eyes wide in anticipation looked nervously around, making sure no one was in sight. He slipped his small hand between the bars to unlatch the lock that secured the bars to the window.

The lock was rusty with age but he had no trouble as the bars swung free. Within minutes the boy deftly slid his switch blade though a gap between the windows and opened the window latch. He slipped inside then gave one last glanced around before pulling the iron bars shut, then the window.

The room was black except for the ray of light of the window. He moved through the dark with familiar ease and headed for the staircase he knew was somewhere to his left. He bumped into something hard and cold and he fought down the panic. It was not there before. Someone else had been here, he thought but he knew reason for it. The building had been condemned for months now. That meant either a homeless person had found shelter or that the city was finally going to demolish the building. In either case someone found his secret.

He made his way around the object and headed for his destination. He went down creaking stairs down into a darker basement. Only now did he turn on his flashlight. Shining the light in a wide arc he looked around, satisfied that all appeared normal. He zeroed the light on the object of his search. It sat quietly against the stone wall. He examined as if a general inspecting his troops.

He closed his eyes, remembering where his mother had gone. Probably to the fruity, scatter-brain neighbor of theirs. He didn't worry about his older brother, who had moved out several months ago. He relaxed in the darkness, knowing no one would miss him for hours.

The rays of the flashlight glinted against the polished chrome. Swirls of dust, invisible in the darkness became visible in the light before disappearing back into the void of blackness. He looked up at the faint noise. He listened intently for several minutes, but heard nothing more. He brought out a soft squirmy object from his duffel bag and set it down on the cold steel. The boy brought the shield down over the puppy's neck, pinning it down. The animal hardly moved despite the danger it sensed.

The boy, a slight grin forming on his face took a deep breath. He looked at the contraption that he found in the basement several weeks ago. With one hand on the lever he looked around as if expecting an audience then pulled on the lever.

The blade at first did nothing and the boy stood in disbelief. His face grew dark with rage and he screamed obscenities at the machine. He kicked the machine finally dislodging the blade. It made only a slight whisper as the blade slid down, followed by a dull clink as the blade bit into flesh, then bone, then wood. The boy watched with elation as the severed head fell without a sound into a basket full of oily rags.

****

The woman wandered among the rocky tide pools, studying or pretending to study the sea anemones, a sea urchin and other sea life. She was also watching out of the corner of her eye, a young man sitting alone on a rock not far from where she was. He was looking out at the steel gray white capped sea. She studied him a moment longer then turned her attention back to the tide pools. She didn't see him approach her from behind.

"How's it going?" he said, startling her.

She spun around and almost fell. She gaped at him foolishly. When the silence continued he began to feel embarrassed.

"Do you live around here?" he asked.

She still didn't answer and he wondered if he should have come over. He started to leave, angry and frustrated at her idiot expression. He was surprised when she found her voice.

"Wait. I didn't mean..." she stammered.

He stopped and turned, forcing himself to calm down. They settled into the usual shallow conversation that two strangers act out. Without realizing it they found themselves walking back to the small beach where Darlene had her beach chair. Dave tried to probe deeper like a swimmer trying to reach the bottom of a pool.

Without warning a friend of Darlene's, who out of loneliness or protection, joined the couple. Darlene excused herself to use the restroom and Maggie seized the opportunity.

"So. How long have you known Dar?" she asked.

"We just met," Dave answered, surprised by the question.

"I think I should tell you something about Darlene. You might think it's none of my business, but she is a good friend," she said. "She had a traumatic experience when she was about thirteen. A group of kids from another neighborhood attacked her, while she

123

was walking back from the beach. I won't go into details, but it left her fearful of strangers and especially men." She spat out the word 'men' with disgust.

Dave glared at her, unsure of her motives. Was she trying to protect her friend or was it out of jealousy of some kind. Darlene seemed normal in their conversation, maybe a little shy. He didn't say anything until Darlene came back.

The three talked a little longer until Maggie, feeling like the third wheel left. He had to tread lightly around Darlene. He was used to the coarse language of his uncle and cousins. Around her though he felt as if he was holding something delicate.

He asked her if she wanted to do something that night and was not surprised when she turned him down saying that she was attending a bible study seminar. The next night she was free and they made the date. When she had left he began to analyze their afternoon.

****

The young man scanned the dimly lit sparsely traveled street, taking in all the important details. Quietly he left the safety of the dark alley, his mind acting like a camera. He took in the old brick buildings, dark reddish in the darkness, and cold in the night. The boarded up store windows reminded the few passerby's of long ago bargains.

He watched the people on the streets with contempt. Their heels clicked in rhythm on the sidewalk, their aimless wandering irritated him for some reason.

They were the same lonely people, night after night going somewhere, attempting to go anywhere and ending up nowhere. Staring at something, but seeing nothing. He wondered who they were, how they lived. He feared and hated them.

He hated the buildings for the same way, since they were also old and forlorn, used up and waiting to perish. He despised them mostly for the fact that he was one of them. Lonely in search of hope, hoping and searching for something better.

His heart skipped a beat, as he thought he saw someone he knew. A further look told him that it was someone else. He paused at a quiet intersection, then turned down a deserted street. He found himself following an elderly man.

The old man suddenly stiffened as if clubbed from behind, then turned around. For some reason he relaxed at the sight of the younger man with the clean, baby face and innocent smile. He turned back and continued on. The old man paused at a dark alley, looked down at the ground as a roll of mucus dripped from his misshapen nose into a salt and pepper beard. With his head down, the old man walked on, when a parked car suddenly turned on its lights. It raced away from the curb with its tires protesting.

The old man temporally blinded by the lights cursed silently at the intrusion. He watched the fading glow of the taillights, then turned around to see where the young man was. He didn't see him and shrugged, his warm alcohol laden breathe evident in the cool night air.

****

The child sat in the noon day sun, mesmerized by the action going on below. His steel gray eyes darted from one contestant to the other. They were barely visible in the dust they threw up in the crude makeshift arena. The boy felt like a proud Roman emperor as he swallowed a handful of grapes and fanned himself with his mother's favorite Japanese fan.

This time he pitted a German shepherd puppy, maybe ten weeks old against a large tom cat. He starved them both on purpose to provoke the fight. A smile erupted on his small face when the bloody battle ended.

He looked upon the winner with pride, since it was his favorite cat. The dog lay whimpering, then was silent as the cat, crazed with hunger started to feed. The boy elated, reached over to pick up the cat.

The animal, not to be denied a meal, swiped the boy on the arm, leaving a deep, ugly gash. The boy let out a screech, dropping the cat, which went back to its meal.

The boy in anger and embarrassment picked up a two by four and brought it down hard on the cat's back. The cat screamed in agony and forgetting its hunger fled for safety. The boy took out the rest of his tantrum on the dead animal, screaming obscenities at it.

The commotion attracted the attention of a passing woman who was walking her dog. She peered through the fence and saw a 10-

year-old boy crying. She immediately felt a maternal sympathy for the boy. The neighbor continued to pull her nervous poodle along, its eyes bulging with fear, its instinct sensing trouble.

****

It was a long, but relaxing drive. The talk flowed freely, not forced. It took a couple of hours as they ascended the narrow valley. The air became cooler and crisper and cleaner. The pines increased as they rose with an occasional aspen that had exploded with reds and yellows.

Dave remembered these mountains as a kid when his father would bring him up here during the summer. It was the middle of the week, so there were no weekend campers and the kids were back in school. Only a solitary hard-core fisherman, trying his luck in the stream that ran along the road.

Dave took the day off from work while Darlene skipped two classes. They drove off the main road onto a dirt road for several miles until he stopped at a meadow. The silence engulfed them, the smells of the wildflowers and the aroma of the pines stung their senses.

With their arms loaded with food and blankets, they made their way across the meadow and found a flat clearing near a clump of pine trees. Dave unfolded the blanket while she set out the food, carefully laying out the jars like pieces on a chess set. He looked at the array of strange multi-colored jars. He relaxed a bit when she brought out a loaf of bread, some cheese and a bottle of burgundy. He opened one of the jars and wrinkled his nose.

"What the hell is this?" he managed to say politely.

"It's asparagus juice and banana yogurt mixed together," she announced giggling at his pantomime of being sick. She started to explain the benefits of the mixture, unaware of the lone figure, who watched their movements from a distance through binoculars.

****

The shadow moved with swift determination along the dark alley. It was too dark to see, but the shadow moved unerringly, through the obstruction of garbage cans and boxes. The young man's breathing was faster than usual. He kept telling himself not to panic, but he failed. He must not fail this time, he thought. The very idea of failure frightened him.

He didn't normally go out two nights in a row. If it wasn't for the stupid car, he thought for the zillionth time. He felt his hand gingerly hoping that it wasn't broken. He had to control his temper. He just couldn't go around punching out brick walls. He would just have to succeed tonight.

He followed another alley that he found a little wider but no less darker. Soon it emptied out into a dimly lit but familiar street, a street he knew from the past. He paused long enough to survey the street.

An old man with a dingy rain coat that came down to his knees, fumbled with something in a trash can. The can flipped over sending the bum onto his stomach and spilling the contents of the trash can on the street.

Grumbling and cursing, the old man slowly rose from the mess, only to be greeted by the young man with an amusing smile and an iron bar in his left hand. The bar came down hard against the bum's temple ending his miserable existence.

The young man hesitated as the bum slumped to the ground. He could hardly catch his breath, when he heard the rough grating noise of tires on asphalt, then the scream of disc brakes as it bit into steel rims.

He turned in horror as he found himself facing a young policeman in a blue and white cruiser. Revolving blue and red lights framed the wide excited eyes of the officer. The two stared at each other for a frozen second, until the young man threw the iron bar at the windshield. The face of the rookie cop disappeared behind the spreading rays of the shattered glass. He turned and ran for the dark alley from which he came. He ran until he was forced to stop, bent over with his hands on his knees. He glanced back expecting to see the cop, but no one was there.

****

The little boy, all eighty-six pounds of him, lay in the dust in the middle of the makeshift arena. He writhed in pain, his mind in chaos. He barely could make out anything except for obscure shapes and forms broken only by a blinding light. Whether the shapes were moving or he was, he couldn't be certain. What he was aware of was the unbearable pain in his forearm and the white-hot pain that inched its way up to his neck. His mind was becoming a battleground of alternating hallucinations and surrealism. The reality of unfocused images and an occasional hint of focused reality all seemed to blend.

One image resembled his mother, large and menacing holding a broom. Another was the sea-green eyes of his brother grinning like an elf. Then his mother returned, who at first smiled with assurance, then changed to a look of scorn or else fear. It was a look not unlike that of the frightened tom cat.

The pain was now affecting his young mind, destroying little by little his senses. The blood, a trickle at first, flowed from his mouth, mixing with a grayish white foam on his pale face. A gust of wind swept across the yard playing with his hair. The boy was not amused despite his expression, since he was quite dead, already attracting flies that also gathered on the other animal nearby.

****

The frightened young girl watched with alarm as the gang approached her slowly out of the darkness. Somewhere from above the hard driving, chaotic beat of punk music filtered down from someone's apartment. The footsteps of the six youths clashed in rhythm with the music. The girl frozen with fear started to back pedal almost tripping over the curb.

One of the six began snapping his fingers to the beat, which seemed louder now. He had a sturdy pocked-mark face, anchored by black eyes and an ugly sneer. Suddenly he pulled a metallic object from his pocket, its steel glinting off the neon lights of the street. With it he made threatening gestures, then like an actor performing an intense love scene, fondled the knife, caressing it gently.

The gang was now more than a few yards from her when they stopped abruptly. She tried to move, but her legs were warm with fear and her feet seemed cemented to the sidewalk. She did not cry out or even whimper, only her eyes revealing terror.

The one with the knife moved silently up to her, inspecting her like a used car. With the knife held loosely in one hand, he brought the other down across her face, sending her reeling to the ground. A flash of pain shot through her as everything in front of her began to swim. The neon lights blinked like seductive eyes.

The six black shapes encircled her. A huge hand made its way out of the unfocused blur and grabbed her from behind and picked her up. The hand shoved her into a massive hairy chest in which equally hairy arms engulfed her. It stank of stale leather, cheap after shave, beer and cigarettes.

The twins, nearly six hundred pounds between them, escorted her to an abandon building across the street. They half dragged her, while the others snickered behind. They entered through a doorless opening into a large room.

The room looked as if it was once the lobby of a hotel. It was a room where the sounds of guests once checked in or out, the ringing of a bell calling for a bellhop and the grinding of an elevator as it ascended or descended. The only sound now was the dull thud of a body being dumped on a dusty old couch.

"Who's first?" someone said, a sound of urgency in his voice.

"Me," grunted one of the bearded twins affixing his gaze on the others in a show of male dominance. The others knew deep down where the real power in the group lay. That lay with the slight figure who stood in the back of the room and whom they called TC even though his real name was Robert.

He didn't look like the type who gave orders much less backed them up. Behind the sea-green eyes rested a power and authority few questioned.

The bearded twin fixed an eye on his brother as the slender one strolled slowly to the girl. He saw that she wasn't more than thirteen or fourteen. He smiled down at her and for a minute the girl saw pity and concern in his eyes but that quickly vanished. He began to finger her blouse and she struggled weakly, but she didn't cry out. Maybe she's retarded and didn't know what was going on, he thought.

It really didn't matter and when he finished, he got up slowly, buttoning his pants and checking his back pocket. The others, huddled in another part of the room, drifted back toward her like fog off the ocean.

TC sat looking at the empty street through a boarded up window. He knew the others would be bluffing, cussing, sneering and even fighting for next in line. He heard the loud grunting and knew one of the twins was next. She still didn't scream or cry out and that puzzled her. Not that it would matter to him anyway. He lit a cigarette and inhaled the harsh smoke, feeling it race to his nerves calming him. He exhaled, obscuring the window with clouds of thought. Why didn't she scream?

****

The young man stood at a distance from the rest of his family as they gathered around the small gravesite. Each figure stiff in shock, each face etched with grief and disbelief. A slight drizzle mixed with the leaden sky. As far away as the man was, he still could hear his mother weeping quietly. His aunt was holding her gently consulting her.

"The good Lord has come and taken him," she was telling her sister.

The young man watched as his aunt guided his mother away from the proceedings. More than once his aunt condemned him to his face, quoting from the Bible. He didn't care what happened two thousand years ago or what treaty someone signed two hundred years ago. He didn't care who invaded who or that x square plus y square equaled z square. Who cared, he asked himself a thousand times. Did it matter that his high school team scored a touchdown? How he managed to graduate, he never knew.

What did matter were his friends, even though three of them were now dead. Two had died from a car crash and someone shot one of the twins in a drive-by shooting. Sex mattered most of all to him. If he couldn't score off a chick by using his alluring charms and good looks, he resorted to forceful means.

He needed to satisfy his expanding thirst for control over people and situations. The odd shape object that he kept in his back pocket, helped him gain that control. It was made of smooth polished marble and was the color of rich cream and shaped like a Greek symbol of lambda. He didn't know what the symbol meant or did he care. What mattered was the control it gave him, the power that seemed to come from nowhere and engulf him completely. He found himself fingering the object.

He watched as the small crowd began to drift away in separate directions. Only then did he find himself moving forward toward the small casket of his brother. He could almost imagine his brother smiling up at him with that insane grin.

He felt no remorse, in fact he was almost elated when he learned

130

the little queer was dead. Queers had always revolted him, sickened him, but that night several months ago when he still lived at home was a blemish, which even the object couldn't remove.

The naked boy had crept into his bed late at night and began fondling the older boy's penis, caressing it and even licking it and finally swallowing the swelling organ in his small mouth.

Waking up to the sudden shock of what was happening, the youth threw the boy off the bed in a fit of rage. The boy landed with a moan, then got back up. The youth caught his brother hard with a blow to his temple sending him to the floor. It took several moments before the shaking of anger and the tears of shame subsided. White with shock, he grabbed his clothes and went out into the night.

When he came back the next morning, his mother asked him where he was. He mumbled something, avoiding her eyes. Her hair was uncombed and her eyes were puffy from crying or lack of sleep or both.

"Where you been?" she whispered in defeat.

She still had her little boy, who she was determined would grow up to be good. Not like his older brother. He fidgeted the object and for some reason, her expression seemed to soften.

He needed to be away from her and especially from him, so he packed his father's old army duffel bag and moved into one of friend's place. As he was leaving, he saw the pale oval face of his brother from the bedroom window. He had an ugly discoloration on one side of his face. He waved at his older brother with an impish grin and like a well-acted play, the curtain closed for good.

****

The young woman woke out of the smoky haze. She lay quietly in the dark, feeling her heart beat, while her fears slowly ebbed away. The dreams came often and she would avoid sleep for fear of it. She could almost smell the stale cigarettes and the cheap beer and panic would set in. A clammy, sticky arm brushed against hers and she jumped in fear. She looked over in relief at him as he tossed quietly in his sleep. She had the dream often, but she never cried out. She didn't then and she wouldn't now.

****

The sprawling campus of the local junior college wasn't well lit, especially the visitors parking lot where he had his Dodge pick-up parked. Despite the poor lighting, he still recognized the girl walking toward him. He remembered the half slouched shuffle, her arms wrapped around her books tightly, her head down covered by the shag of blonde hair. She was not the same as before and yet she was. He saw her face and knew it was her. Six years doesn't erase the memory of her mute stare, full of hatred and coldness that he couldn't comprehend.

As she neared, the facial features became familiar, the narrow set eyes, the small nose and the lean but soft face. She could really be attractive if she wanted to. He got out of the truck and followed her. He was right behind her, trying not to appear as if he was in a hurry.

She didn't seem to notice him at first, then all the sudden she stopped, almost colliding into him. Recovering in time, he grunted an apology and continued past her unsure of what to do. He finally stopped, turned and faced her and found her glaring at him. It was the same coldness from the past.

They stood facing each other for what seemed a lifetime before she turned and ran. Catching up to her, he tackled her into the bushes. He managed to pin her down, before she had a chance to fight back.

She didn't fight back. She just laid there without a sound, her pale face partially obscure by her hair. The only sound was her heavy breathing and her icy stare, which seemed ear piercing.

For a brief moment, he felt a sort of fear crept through him. Not fear of her, but of the hatred that emanated from her eyes.

Reality set back in as he felt the power surge back into him. He had the knife and he had the object in his pocket. The power ripped through him and he ripped at her clothes exposing her breast, then slipping his hand down her unbuttoned jeans. He never really had a true girlfriend. He dated and slept with many women, but they were all nameless faces to him. An endless procession of hair and flesh. He felt the wet warmth of the soft hair and the unbelievable softness of her thighs. He exploded into eagerness of pain and pleasure as he fumbled with his own jeans.

Suddenly a pair of headlights swept into view blinding them both for a moment. In panic, he got up and fumbled his way deeper into the bushes, away from the light. Pulling up his pants he turned and saw her standing there among the branches. He disappeared into obscurity like a shadow into darkness.

****

Dave pulled into the lot, unprepared for the sight of her emerging from the bushes, her clothes torn, and her hair in disarray. What stunned him was the calm aloof expression, as she kept looking over her shoulder. He ran up to her, but her expression never changed.

"What the hell happened?" he screamed into her face, rage and injustice raging in his eyes.

She only glared at him without emotion. He ran past her into the park, but saw nothing except the eerie shapes of trees and bushes. He returned to the car and finding her in the front seat, put his jacket over her. They were far from the campus, before she began to sob quietly.

****

He knew he shouldn't be there especially in this neighborhood. He had no choice, because he had to stay clear of his own. He knew the cops would be hanging around asking questions. At first he didn't see them, only hearing the click-clacking of their heels on the concrete. From out of the darkness they appeared. He wished he listened to his instincts rather than his fears. He thought maybe they wouldn't see him if he blended into the darkness of the alley.

He felt for the knife and his stomach twisted into knots when he realized it was gone. He felt for the object, but it too was gone. He tried to calm himself by thinking ahead, planning his next moves. He must have lost the object and the knife in the struggle with the girl. Fear and doom crept through him like a wicked disease. He wished that his own gang was around. Even having one of the twins with him would make a difference.

"Hey shit face," taunted one of the kids and the rest laughed. "Whatcha doing out so late? The retirement home too crowded."

He was slender and held an iron bar. They were almost on him and he could see their leering, sneering, angry faces. Six angry thugs spitting vile. The tallest and heaviest moved close to him, his small

133

black eyes full of hatred, his pudgy chin jutted out in challenge.

Without a word, the pudgy kid swung hard catching him in the pit of the stomach. It was as if someone extracted all the air away leaving him gasping in pain. Another blow caught him just above his sea-green eyes, knocking him to the cold hard street. He swung at the swirling dark forms above him, but he only heard laughing. Someone with a strong grip lifted him up and for a brief second, he thought it was one of the twins, but he knew that they were dead.

More blows rained down on him and he thought of the girl. He heard rather than felt his nose break and the warm liquid streaming on his face.

He never saw the icy hot blade of the knife, but he felt the searing heat of the incision in the pit of his stomach. He tried to breathe, but only felt the searing sucking pain as the blade was thrusted upwards. He knew he was near the end and he welcomed the calm darkness that invaded his soul. The physical pain slowly decreased as he fell to the ground one last time.

The End

LONELY POEM

The apartment looked so empty to him, but he could not think of anything to add to make the place more comfortable. He studied the plain but durable couch, upholstered in a lime green Scottish pattern. He knew he needed a matching chair.

He looked around the room, at the light brown carpet and the tan drapes, all looking so drab. Maybe he needed another table or a lamp in the corner next to the small television. No, he thought, he could not afford that.

He studied the desk with the computer keyboard partially covered with a newspaper. Books sat above the desk on a cheaply made book shelf. A dictionary and a thesaurus anchored one end of the shelf while copies of westerns filled the rest.

A full waste basket sat on the floor next to the desk like a lost puppy catching any over flows from the desk. It seemed to compliment the computer, the beginning and the end, the start and the finish.

He studied the small stereo that faced the television. Newspapers lay scattered on the floor in the middle of the room. Magazines lay exposed on the couch.

The room still didn't seem right but he gave up playing interior decorator. No one came here anyway, he thought. Besides he already lost interest in the room. He had a habit of quickly losing interest in things.

He once wrote to the National Geographic Society, expecting them to send him on an assignment to some far off land. A polite, but formal form letter arrived rejecting his offer of employment. He wondered if any one actually read his letter.

The letter was probably the butt of some jokes during lunch hour among the secretaries and editors at the National Geographic headquarters.

It was still a dream of his. A mind is always healthier when it is fed nourishing quests. Even if they did send him on an assignment, he probably would lose interest in it.

He looked at himself in the full length hall mirror that hung at the end of the short and cluttered hallway. To the right was a small cluttered bedroom and to the left was a small cluttered bathroom.

He studied himself in the mirror, the short gray hair, not quite a crew cut, but definitely not long either. His hard granite like face was not handsome, but not unattractive either.

Deep eyebrows hid deep set blue eyes. A sharp straight nose divided his face equally. A gray stab of a mustache sat at the foot of his nostrils. His teeth were slightly stained from years of coffee and a long stint with cigarettes. He was fifty-eight and patted his protruding belly, flexing his sinewy muscles on his arms.

The phone rang which startled him. He went to pick it up, but it went dead by the time he got there.

He shrugged feeling antsy to get out of the apartment. He grabbed his favorite sweater from the cluttered dresser, then patted his pockets to make sure he had his keys. He stopped in the living room as if deciding his destination.

It was Saturday and people jammed the street. He revealed in the fresh spring air as he hobbled down the steps to the street.

Joggers ran by in their expensive colorful warm-ups and multi-colored running shoes. Several of the joggers, mostly the younger ones, wore headsets hooked into invisible stereos, their heads bobbing with the beat.

An elderly woman walked by, her expression in contradiction with the sunny day. She weaved through the crowd, clutching her hand bag with white gnarled hands.

A young woman, her blonde hair flowing freely behind her came in the opposite direction. She smiled at the stares from the men around her including Harold, who stared at the thin tank top. She wore a long flowered skirt that flowed around her long legs like waves at the beach. The young woman passed the old woman without looking at her, her smile hardening just a little. When she passed Harold her features soften again.

The old woman looked back with a look of remorse. A look of long ago was evident in her eyes. Harold knew that look. The old woman had walked the same streets as a young woman and smiled at the men, possibly Harold. Now she was old and gray. She stopped and waited as Harold walked by, still looking back at the girl.

"You should be ashamed of yourself. Mr. Foster," she said.

"Good morning to you to Mrs. Bryant," he called after her. "...You, old bag of fart," he muttered to himself. He grinned at her broad back before he turned away.

A large middle-age woman with an unattractive face walked by. She had several sagging chins and stringy dark red hair, which she tied in a bun on top of her head. She dragged along three poodles, each going in separate directions. The dogs growled at the passersby with their short, shrill little barks.

The dogs were only good for trolling behind a Chris craft in shark infested waters, Harold thought. He hated poodles as he watched one of the little shark baits relieve itself on a fire hydrant.

The woman seemed embattled not with the dogs but with slicing her way through life. Her reddish face flushed with the strain.

Harold stopped at the bus stop at the corner of his street and a larger street. He looked at his watch, then glanced in the direction of the bus.

"Late as always," the voice behind him said.

He turned to the smiling face of a middle-age black woman. She held what looked like a sewing bag under her arm.

Harold forced a smile but said nothing. He checked his watch again only out of nervous habit. He finally spotted the multi-colored bus plastered with ads several blocks away.

It stopped at the light, then switched lanes to pass, then back into the right lane, where it stopped with a swoosh and the groan of brakes and finally the clunk of the hydraulic doors. The doors opened, emitting the passengers like sewage.

The black woman got on, followed by a young kid with curly black hair and faded blue jeans. Harold got on next, dropping two quarters in the plastic tank. A bored driver sat in his seat, peaking into the rear view mirror, before shutting the doors again with a swish.

The bus pulled away with a jerk before Harold found a seat, almost causing him to stumble. He sat next to a thin, odd looking man in his late twenties. He had thin blonde hair that was receding at the temples. His large pointed nose seemed to compliment his nervous eyes. The man glanced around quickly at Harold, before shifting back to the back of the seat.

Harold looked at the back of the seat as well as if he was missing something. He let his attention wander over the backs of the bobbing heads in the seats in front of him.

He glanced toward the back of the bus and saw a young boy of around fifteen embracing an even younger girl. She wore make up and looked much older, if not less attractive. No one paid attention to the two lovers in the back. A bearded man slept directly in front of the lovers. His long gray hair drooped like a dead plant over his thin shoulders. It partially covered his thin yellowish face. His head bobbed with the motion of the bus. He slept as if he had not slept in days.

Harold's attention shifted to the nervous blonde man sitting next to him. His hands seemed to be in constant motion, adjusting his silver rimmed glasses, fingering his ear as if to get the water out of them. He stroked his chin, then went back to his glasses. Harold figured he wanted to pick his nose, but knew he was in public.

Harold didn't belong with these slobs. He knew he was better than them. The bus came to a lurching stop, waking up the sleeping man. He glanced out the dirty windows to see where he was. Satisfied, he nodded off to sleep again.

An obese woman got on the bus, looking from the left to the right for a seat, slowly easing her body down the narrow aisle. A young man with a backpack waited impatiently behind her. He peered over her also looking for an elusive seat. He was a thin man with black rim glasses, which seemed to magnify his eyes. His black greasy hair fell in ringlets almost to his shoulder. Finally, the fat woman sat down in an open seat with a resounding thud. The young man behind her looked around in panic before spotting a seat next to the sleeping man.

The youth glanced at the lovers with a sigh before he sat down. He forged his attention elsewhere. The lovers never seemed to stop as they seemed to be sucking their faces dry. The boy slipped his hand in and out of her blouse while she played with his crouch.

Harold felt angry at being in the middle of this menagerie of lovers and losers. He hated these people even more. The moving panorama of the city streets and concrete canyons and the non-stop traffic, all seemed to blur fading in and out between reality and clarity and illusion. The people seemed to whirl around this hellish merry-go-round. It seemed like an endless nightmare.

Harold rose suddenly, not because he needed to, but because he wanted to. He felt an ache in his chest and pitched forward, not seeing whom he fell on. All he remembered was the fat lady standing over him with her large painted-on blue eyes. She faded away almost before the screaming started from the large cavernous mouth of hers.

****

Harold found himself near a lake. He was lying on his back on a blanket. He rose and looked around the lake and the surrounding landscape. The air was warm like a summer wind. The sun, bright, shone through the full bloom of the oak tree.

The lake was not large, more like a pond with a clump of lily pads along one side of it. The water erupted in small boils as trout rose up and fed on small insects that alit on the water or fell from the trees.

Harold saw no one around and got to his feet. He made his way down to the water and looked at his reflection. What he saw made him jump back in fright. The reflection was a much younger version of himself. The face was thirty years younger.

A woman called to him and he spun around. He saw a beautiful young woman of around twenty-two approach him. Her soft blonde hair fell onto her shoulders like a gentle waterfall and her face shone with an ivory complexion.

Her dark blue eyes beamed bright with happiness, her face flushed with joy. She waved as she came closer, then stopped when she came up to him. In a flash she disappeared, only to be replaced by an angry young man with a scar on his right cheek.

The man had a look of anger as he bellowed out the insults, which seemed to hurt more than the feeble blows that followed. Harold doubled up to protect himself. When he recovered, he saw a young boy staring up at him. The boy had been crying. His face puffy from the swelling, his lip bloody.

The mirror went blank as he stared over at the girl who lay next to him in bed. It was dark and she was sobbing, her back to him. He saw his hand reach over to comfort her but she pulled away and he didn't know why. He didn't want her to cry and told her so, but the crying continued. She slowly faded away into the darkness.

Suddenly the lights blinded him and the smell gagged him.

"He's coming to," a voice said. It was a female voice and for a minute he thought they were angels. Harold opened his eyes and peered into the dark eyes of a man in a white coat. At that moment, for some reason he thought God had blue eyes. The man hovered over him with professional intent.

"We thought you were a goner," he said, pulling open Harold's eye wider.

Harold looked around the sterile room. Someone had closed a green curtain around one of the beds across from him. He heard a raspy breathing behind the curtain. The other two beds were empty. Each bed had a chair next to it. There were two televisions on each wall facing the beds.

Harold ignored the doctor who checked his heart with an icy cold stethoscope. Finally, he was aware of the tube that protruded from his arm.

"Mr. Foster?" the doctor asked with practiced skill "You had a mild stroke. Your blood pressure is very high. Do you smoke?"

Harold shook his head.

"Good. Also you have to..."

Harold didn't listen. He did not care if his blood pressure went through the roof. He looked at a vase of plastic flowers on a small table by one of the beds. He looked at his own empty table and was depressed. The doctor had stopped talking and was giving him a strange look. The doctor looked around forty. What was he doing at forty? Harold thought. Lori was still alive. So was Jeff.

"Cars." Harold said to himself.

How he hated cars, especially the little foreign ones. He could not bring himself to remember Jeff at twenty. He did remember him at eight. Jeff beaming from under his red baseball hat. An eight-year-old smile that separated the sea of freckles.

The old man smiled at his son's home run but he didn't show it to his son. The boy didn't even detect a small hint of pride as he skipped away to rejoin his team mates. Jeff grew up never expecting encouragement or affection from his father. Harold regretted not telling the boy that he was proud of him.

The little boy faded from memory only to be replaced by the face of the doctor. The doctor thumbed his eye back again and shined a beam of light. The doctor grunted something, then left among a flurry of nurses, who checked behind the closed curtain.

Later that night, alone in the darkness, he heard the wheezing from behind the curtain. Harold turned back to the past, but could not remember anything. He fell asleep with relief.

****

He was gone only for a week, but his apartment looked so alien to him. A collection of mail and newspapers cluttered the hallway that led to his door. He tried the key, jiggling it a little, before opening the door to a musty living room. A feeling of fear gripped him. A feeling of isolation clogged his thinking, clouding his memory.

A foul odor stabbed at his senses, awaking his back to reality. The odor came from the direction of the kitchen. He saw the lettuce on the counter turning into a black mess. He poured out the milk and tossed the lettuce and anything else that did not look right. He needed to make a trip to the store.

He felt annoyed and slammed the refrigerator door. He made his way to the living room, eerie in eternal silence. He thought about buying new furniture. Maybe even a DVD recorder for the television. He could start writing again. He was determined now to write. He could write articles for the trade magazines, maybe a little fiction.

He sat on the couch and thought of all the things he could do. Tomorrow he thought. Today he would rest. He closed his eyes, the noises of the street, slowly fading as did the daylight. He fell into a slumber and the dreams came back to his tired mind.

The dreams came like waves on a beach. Short and without meaning. Dreams that were soon forgotten. In one dream, someone was chasing him down a deserted dark street. He didn't see who it was, but he knew he had to run. He saw shadows dancing like wild children on the gray concrete walls. No form materialized from the shadows.

He looked down seeing for the first time, the gun in his hand. He stared at it then at the approaching danger. He grew tired of running so he turned and faced the danger. He pointed the gun but it wouldn't fire.

He couldn't squeeze the trigger and he began to panic. He gave up and backed away, the gun still pointing at the menace. He didn't know what it was but he knew he had to flee. He yelled for it to stop and when it didn't he woke in a bath of sweat. It took a moment for him to realize where he was.

Ominous shapes seemed to form from the darkness. The shapes faded and became familiar objects in his room. He suddenly realized that he was running from himself. He was staring at himself.

He laid back down, his head in pain. He hated to be alone, yet when he was in people's presence he grew weary of them.

He always felt trapped, wishing he was somewhere else. He wished life was like a book or television. If he grew tired of the characters he would turn the page or turn off the television. If he grew lonely, all he needed was to pick up a book or turn on the television.

The morning was suddenly there, as if he knew it would be. He woke when the alarm went off. He didn't know why he still kept setting the alarm, since he was retired. He rose and looked out the barred windows into the alley behind his building. He made his way to the bathroom where he studied himself in the water stained mirror and realized the face in his dream stared back at him. He splashed water on his face, searching for his tooth brush.

The living room looked the same as before and he decided to go outside. The people around him did not seem to exist to him. He felt so much older than a week ago.

A young girl flew by on roller blades, listening to music through her headsets. Her shoulder length, brown hair trailed behind her. She passed him, her mouth forming the words to the silent song.

Harold headed for the park, which he knew to be several blocks away. He passed two tennis courts, side by side in misuse.

A group of teenagers played street ball on the courts. Several tough looking middle-age men, stood and watched them.

Toward the middle of the park was a semi-circular pattern of benches where an old man sat, feeding a flock of birds. A derelict in dirty clothes slept in a fetal position, near two graffiti covered bathrooms.

Harold sat down on a bench across from the old man and his birds. Another man, a middle age man in a rumpled business suit sat nearby. He looked as if slept in the suit. He thumbed through a newspaper, his face one with concern.

Two other men hunched over a chess game deep in thought. Neither of the chess players looked up as Harold walked up to them. After several tense moments, one of them made a move and looked up with a triumphal smile.

"That looks like trouble for your queenie, Jimmy old boy," said the one chess player.

He looked at Harold as if for the first time and winked.

Harold nodded, studying the board and realizing the game was almost over. The other man, still hunched over, bored into his remaining pieces as if expecting them to move.

"You lousy faggot," Jimmy finally spoke. "I always knew you were the queen."

The victor laughed, unaware that Harold had moved away.

"How about a game?" he said to Harold's back.

Harold had turned back and shook his head politely.

"I'm not through with you, you shit brain queer," the loser said.

He glared across the board at his past and future opponent.

With his queen about to be taken, leaving only the king and a few pawns, he looked at his opponent's almost intact army. He swung his arm across the table, knocking over the pieces. He got up in anger and stormed off.

"I apologize for my brother. He'll be back," the winner said with a smile.

"I hardly ever play," Harold lied.

"You can't be any worse than he is," the man said.

He pointed in the direction of his older brother.

"And I'm sure you don't have his temper."

"No thanks. Maybe another day. I come here often," Harold said.

"Okay," the winner said with a shrug. "We're usually here."

As Harold drifted away, he passed a young couple pushing a stroller. There was a pink bundle of flesh buried in a blue blanket. The couple was talking quietly to each other.

Memories continued to flash through Harold's mind. The painful past resurfaced like a long sunk submarine.

He walked faster, trying to outrun the memories. Flashes of a young blonde woman holding an infant, seared his mind. The woman placed the baby on a blanket, a blue blanket and smiled at him. They sat in a green meadow by a lake. The woman was very beautiful, her golden hair fell graceful to her shoulders.

She got up and started to walk toward him, glancing over her shoulder at the infant. Harold watched her come toward him, her long legs barely visible beneath the paisley summer dress. As she came nearer, her face grew older with every step. She was almost to him and he saw that she was now old and gray. Suddenly she vanished and he looked around. He called out her name as people looked at him in confusion.

He saw the baby on the blanket. The infant was occupied with something in its tiny fists. Suddenly the baby was gone, leaving only the blanket.

He looked around to see who owned the blanket and when he looked back, he saw the young couple place the baby on the blanket. They both smiled at the infant.

Harold continued on down the path, finding himself back at the circular plaza where the chess winner had found someone else to play.

Harold walked slowly back to his building passing the same faces he seen every day. He stopped in front of his building and looked up at it.

"Go away or I'll call the cops," a middle age woman said.

Her hair was trapped in pink curlers and her face bore a permanent sneer. She lived two stories above him, yet she didn't recognize him. She brushed past him and disappeared into the building.

Harold walked up to his own apartment, the newspaper still scattered on the floor. The kitchen was still cluttered with dirty dishes.

Harold dropped to his knees in front of the oven as if in prayer. With a lot of effort, he pulled down the greasy oven door. A small blue light flickered on the bottom near the broiler, then went out when he blew on it.

He nestled close to the oven and turned the knobs, hearing the hissing of the gas. He felt dizzy and his eyes began to blur.

The visions came back. Of the beautiful blonde woman holding the baby, his baby. A teenage boy with hope in his eyes as a set of car keys was dropped into his eager hands. Slowly the visions began to fade away replaced by a violent orange glow as the explosion ripped through the apartment complex.

The End

A PROBLEM NOT SOLVED

"Nice day huh?" he said, tilting his face to the sun.

"Yeah," she answered obviously bored. She shifted her position on the blanket.

"How was the concert?" she asked.

"It was great except some idiot started a fight with Quinn."

"I thought Quinn's a girl?"

"She is," he answered. "So was the idiot."

He smiled, now more relaxed. She did not show any emotion.

"Is she all right?" she asked not looking at him.

"I guess," he said, amused by the image. "She broke a tooth is all."

They watched two jet skis whined their way through the small surf. They skied in and back out, jumping the breakers.

"What are you going to do?" he asked interrupting her thoughts.

She seemed annoyed at the intrusion and did not bother to hide the fact. "Don't worry about it, okay. You worry too much."

"No I don't."

"And don't whine," she snapped, not caring anymore. "I hate it when you whine."

"Forget it," he said.

"How can I forget it?" she snapped. "It's happening to me." She saw the hurt in his eyes regretting her tone.

"I know. I know."

"Jesel wezel," she said shaking her head.

He turned away, his head down.

"Look. Just don't worry about it," she offered.

"Sure," he managed to say.

A gull skimmed over the water looking for scraps of food to feed on. He envied the bird for its simple life and freedom.

"Look, don't worry for the umpteenth time," she repeated. "Put some lotion on my back will you," she asked holding out the bottle.

She turned over on her stomach and waited for him to pour out the banana smelling liquid. It flowed slowly onto his palm and he laughed.

"You're gross," she smirked, looking back at him. He rubbed the lotion on her silky smooth skin.

"On the shoulders," she ordered. "Ah yeah. There too," she cooed. She squirmed slightly.

"I'll get a job for the summer to pay for it," he said.

"Don't..."

"I know. Don't worry about it but I can't help it," he interrupted. "I called last night. Where were you?"

She did not answer. A slight blush invaded her face but he didn't see the reaction.

"I can't wait till I get my own place," she said finally. "My mom is really..." she didn't finish, instead shaking her head.

"Why don't you move out. You're working."

"I keep telling you that I can't leave her with that lousy... She needs me," she said.

As she talked, his attention shifted to a couple who were jogging along the beach. The girl wore a tight halter top and running shorts. The blonde youth wore only running shorts. They both wore Nikes on the hard sand. The girl's dirty blonde hair, tied in a ponytail, flapped behind her. Her face was alive and radiant.

"Let's do something tonight," he said suddenly.

"I can't. My mom wants me home. Besides it's a school night."

"So?"

"So," she shot back hating that word. "Jeesel weezel. Why don't you just drop it. You're such a drag sometimes. It's gotten to be where you are only good for one...." she stopped.

"What?" he said, not really aware what she was saying.

"I didn't mean that," she said. "Yes I did," she whispered. She rose, angry at him and at herself.

"Lynn wait."

He jumped up, but she did not stop as she gathered her things and walked to her car. He sat back down almost in tears. The gull flew over him without effort unconcern of the human emotions. Its only concern was the warm current of air under its wing that enabled it to rise.

****

She sat in the bleachers and watched with little interest the players on the field. One girl maneuvered her way down the field, the ball going from one foot to the other. She eluded her opponents, then passed to a teammate who kicked it on the run. The ball skirted past the goalie and she let out a cry. The girl on the bleachers did not show any emotions, her thoughts elsewhere.

"Lynn. Come play." A skinny girl ran up to her, out of breath.

"I don't feel well," she said.

"Come on. Don't be a wimp," the other teased but Lynn shook her head.

"Wimpy Lynny."

"I told you, shit head, that I don't want to," Lynn snapped. The other girl stepped back as if slapped.

"We all get them," the girl said walking away.

"What?"

"Cramps. The other girl said over her shoulder.

"Yeah right," Lynn said then got up and ran after the girl.

****

The boy knew what he had to do. He stared hard at the shining razor. He pressed it against his skin. It was cold and his hands shook as he grasped the blade with a tighter grip. He looked into the steamy mirror, startled to see the pale sweaty image return its ghostly gaze.

He pressed down on the blade, not wanting to physically but needing to mentally. He thought of the note, going over it in his tormented mind. It accused the girl of everything, from viciousness, selfishness and disloyalty. It also made quick reference to his few possessions and their intended destinations.

He thought back to when he first met the girl. It was at the beach, the same beach that they were at today. It was one of those incidents that happen too fast. Before they knew it, their relationship grew quickly.

The first few weeks being the happiest of his young life. Then reality set in. The quick flashes of temper, the physical attraction

147

subsiding. Then he saw her kissing someone else. He remembered the numbness, then the hurt that wouldn't go away.

He knew that he couldn't function anymore. Too young to know that time would heal, but he was too impatient. He knew that he couldn't summon the courage without the help of alcohol and some pills he found. He felt relief to find it easier than he thought as he got to that point of no return.

The blade severed the skin and the blood flowed. With a shaky hand he did the same with the other wrist. Then he slumped to the edge of the tub and watched calmly as the life flowed from him.

****

"Come on and play."

"Cripes. Hold on to your bra," Lynn said. "I'm here ain't I? Let's just fucking play," She said taking the goalie's position.

The rest of the girls started to kick the ball down field. The girl felt another cramp. Not a sharp pain but rather an annoyance. She ignored it, as the two groups of girls came back down the field toward her. Her natural instincts told her to move and she did.

The opponent kicked the ball and she reached out to block it. The ball careened off her fist and went out of bounds. She fell to her knees feeling no pain. The skinny girl ran after the ball and brought it back into play. There was a mad scramble for the ball as slender young legs fought for position.

"I got it," someone said.

A girl broke out of the mass and headed for Lynn. The other girl kicked it and again Lynn blocked it in front of her. She did not see the leg that came out of nowhere to kick the rebound. It seemed like an unreal slow motion dream.

As the leg came down in a slow arc, it struck the ball square but it also caught Lynn in the mid-section. The ball squirted into the goal zone and the other team began to celebrate. Lynn doubled up in pain.

"Jesus. Are you okay?" someone asked, the voices piercing the fog.

"You okay Lynny?" came another voice of concern.

"Shit no. Help me up," Lynn said with a grimace.

"I'm going home. I feel shitty," she announced to no one.

"Ah, wimp face."

"What?" she screamed at the crowd. "Who said that. Teri, you fat slut," she cried, going after the girl and ignoring the pain.

A couple of the other girls held her back. Frustrated she stomped away.

"What's eating her?" someone said while everyone shrugged.

****

The girl lay in a bath of sweat. The pain was increasing in tempo. It subsided then increased again. She knew something was deadly wrong. At first, she thought it was her appendix. With a trace of panic and a hint of relief she knew what it was. She had to go for help, a doctor, but that meant money and then her mom would know.

For a moment she thought of calling him. He couldn't even take care of himself and she dismissed the idea.

She made her way to the bathroom where her own image shocked her even more. The pain doubled her over. She was so glad no one was home. She felt her insides change and she felt sick. She looked down at her nightie and saw the blood. She thought of punching herself or getting a coat hanger, then realized that it might not be necessary.

She felt the shift of her bowel movements and the blood flowed. After a while she got up from the toilet and got sick at what she saw. She fumbled to flush it away. She watched in horror as it slowly sucked down into the plumbing.

The End

IRVING

The first evidence of the sun was a light glow far beyond the mountains to the east. To the west, the sky was still inky black, a deep black that reminded Irving of his wife's eyes.

Irving always loved to get up before the sun and watch the silent sky and the quiet neighborhood. His wife hated the inconvenience of his schedule, up at four or five and in bed by eight or nine. Then there were the occasional naps in between.

She thought her own schedule was more sensible, up at ten or eleven, in bed by midnight or when the late show was over. She loved her husband of over forty years, putting up with the increasing annoying habits.

His habit of chewing on the end of the shuffle board stick during matches with other couples or taking his dentures out at the communities' cafeteria or at someone's home for dinner.

"They make my gums itch," he would complain later whenever she brought it up.

"Take them over to Mikes to get them adjusted," she would counter.

DDS Mike Mortberry was the valley's resident dentist. A short, stocky man with over size ears, which dominated his oddly-shaped head. Despite his ears the man was almost deaf and he would have to stand face to face with whomever he was talking to. He was one of Irving's best friends and sometimes partner during the men's tournaments on Thursday's nights.

Because of the smallness of the community, everyone knew every else. Everyone had hordes of friends and Irving Snodgrass and his wife were no exception. Among some of their closest friends besides the Mortberrys were the Bulls, Jerry and Mabel; Bill and Gert Hornblaster and their next door neighbors Hailey and Dick 'nine ball' Nitdwit on one side and Hailey and Harry Bailey on the other. Harry Bailey, considered Irving closest friend, was the community's resident comedian because of his inane and annoying jokes aimed at everyone around him.

No one escaped his humor except for the Nitdwits, who because of their tempers, Bailey as well as most of the residents of the valley stayed away from.

Irving's thoughts were not on Bailey but on the Nitdwits, whom he considered a little odd. They were friendly to Irving at least but still odd, especially Dick Nitdwit. Smacking his lips, another habit that tested his wife's patience, he thought back to prior experiences with Dick 'Nine ball' Nitdwit.

They called him 'Nine ball' because of experiences of not being able to finish nine holes of golf without throwing at least one tantrum, usually breaking on or more of his clubs or throwing his balls in a water hazard.

One incident was when he was fishing in Blue River, which was also the name of the retirement community, when a group of 'young whippersnappers' as he called it, crossed upstream on horseback from where he was fishing. He got so mad at the 'young punks,' actually a group of fifty-year-old newcomers, which he started screaming obscenities and throwing dead trout at them in the middle of the stream. He even hit one in the back with a ten-inch brown.

The horse riders were aghast and managed to beat a hasty retreat except for the lone rider who had a hard time reining his horse and wiping fish guts off him.

When 'Nine Ball' returned to the community center, he wore a triumph grin on his seventy-four-year-old face. He was minus his hundred and forty-dollar fly rod and reel and most of his fish. Dick told the story to anyone who would listen. Irving heard the story himself at least a half dozen times. He was convinced that Dick had old-timer's disease. Hailey would listen intently to every telling of the story from her husband and beam proudly.

Irving grew bored with Dick and his stories and shifted his mind to other incidents that have happened over sixty-nine years of living. He was slowly conscious of the sun, which finally was peeking over the jagged mountains to the east. The light slowly revealed a well-manicured lawn bordered by railroad ties. Flowers surrounded their mobile home on three sides and a lone cottonwood stood next to a wooden fence that separated him from his neighbor.

"Irving," came a loud feminine screech.

"The stupid sun has come up. Pleeease come back to bed before you catch a cold," the singsong voice shattered the stillness.

He didn't bother to acknowledge his wife and imagined her peeking out of the bedroom window at her statue like husband.

His mind erased her voice and thought of Hailey Nitdwit, Dick's wife. One incident that convinced Irving of her oddity was at a party thrown by the Taylor's who lived down the street. Bert was a so-called health food nut, since he was always peddling his three-speed, three-wheel bike around and around the neighborhood. He rode almost as fast as a person walking at normal speed until he tired and spent the rest of the day sitting in a beach chair next to his door as if he was just waiting to die.

His wife also had a bike but she wouldn't ride it after a maiden voyage turned into a Titanic-like crash. Instead of an iceberg it was a palm tree that suddenly jumped out in front of her. She fell head first into a rose bush and never rode again.

Anyway, the party they threw at the community center was going along smoothly when Hailey Nitdwit's drinking got out of hand. Those around her claimed she was drinking a mixture of rum and Gatorade but she violently insisted that they were strawberry daiquiris. Still she managed to disrupt the entire party and made a few lifelong enemies as well.

The result was several people accidentally knocked into the Olympic size pool fully clothed, including the wife of Blue Valley's mayor, Pearl Skylark. Bob Skylark who was a used car salesman could do nothing since he was also afraid of Dick Nitdwit's temper.

He could only watch as Hailey stormed off drunkenly before helping his wife out of the pool. Her hair looked like a deflated blue volleyball that drooped down around her forehead and ears.

Hailey also managed to punch Truman Ivanchek, the black waiter, in the stomach before storming off. She claimed Truman made a racial slur and demanded that he be fired. Ivanchek vehemently denied the charge as accused her of being a racist, which she was since her family was former plantation owners from Mississippi.

The mayor, unable to face up to the Nitdwits was forced to fire the waiter, the reason being his inability to hold a tray upright.

Shocked Truman left and filed a discrimination lawsuit against the community in Tucson. Despite several men holding Mrs. Nitdwit back, she still managed to throw something in his general direction.

Right after the incident, someone claimed they saw her throw the Taylor's' cat against the wall. No one would dare come forward and accuse her of that either. She finally passed out on a lounge chair, much to the relief of everyone, except her husband, who watched the proceedings from behind a wine glass. He wore a crusty grin, whenever he had reasons to be proud.

Irving, recollecting that eventful night, smacked his lips loudly, which seemed to bring him out of his trance. He felt something brush against his leg and looked down to discover his wife's nine-year-old poodle, Fifi, which he totally despised.

The dog was sitting back on its hind legs and holding its paw affectionately, signaling that it was hungry. It was a clever trick that his wife taught the dog.

Irving looked down at the animal with mixed feelings. He always hated the dog, especially since her late brother gave her the animal for her fifty-sixth birthday. He also couldn't stand its constant yapping to go outside, come inside, to be fed, etc. He even felt intolerance toward his wife since she got the dog. He did feel sorry for it as he peered beyond the dog's tiny black eyes into its primitive walnut size brain. The dog just glared back stupidly, uncertain what to do.

Finally, it gave a loud yap, which erased any sympathy Irving had for the pet. He felt the urge to kick it, but restrained for the countless time. The dog sensing hostility from the large form in front of it, went back to the concrete patio, next to the glass sliding door and lay on the hard cold surface. Its ears sprung to life when the glass door then the screen door opened and a more familiar shape, stepped from the darkness and headed toward the larger shape.

Irving saw his wife coming over toward him and he rolled his eyes, letting out a soft moan.

"Irving." came the familiar voice, not unlike the yapping of the dog. "I have breakfast cooking. Come in and eat before we go..."

"Go?" thought Irving. "Go where?" He sifted his mind for the answer bit couldn't come up with one.

"You know how you are when you play on an empty stomach

and you sho..."

"Go where?" snapped Irving.

"Did you forget again? I swear in your old age..."

"Never mind that. Just tell me what it is I forgot." he interrupted, this time more harshly.

His wife stared at him with a shocked expression then finally said softly.

"We're playing golf with the Baileys." She stopped to let that sink in. "Now go inside and eat." she said even more softly.

"Okay. Sure," he moaned, annoyed at being disturbed.

His wife was about to say something, but changed her mind. She swept past the dog and went back into the darkness again.

The dog showed its emotion by wagging its tail. It sensed hostility from Irving as well as an unusual smell and cowered away from him. It trotted happily over to a clump of dead weeds and urinated. Relieved, it trotted even happier back to the patio where it lay down again to wait patiently for its meal.

****

"Nice shot" said Mrs. Bailey as the foursome watched the flight of the ball. It traveled a total of 85 yards before coming to a rest in the thick transplanted grass.

"I didn't slice it the way Mr. Woods told me to," whined Irving's wife, still in her back swing. Mrs. Bailey, out of the corner of her eye could see Irving put his hand to his face. Her own husband rolled his eyes toward the heavens.

"Did you keep your eye on the ball?" offered Mrs. Bailey in a professional tone.

Mr. Bailey holding back a smirk went over and set his ball up on the extra-long white tee. He fumbled with it, patiently trying to balance the ball on it. Finally succeeding he straightened up and swung the club back and forth like a baseball played would. He lined the ball and with a serious face spoke.

"How do you do?"

"What?" Irving snapped.

"I asked how it was," Bailey smirked, looking up from the ball. Irving eyed him warily, shaking his head.

"I'm addressing the ball," Bailey laughed at his own joke. No one else cracked a smile. Of course no one ever even so much as cracked a smile at his jokes. He still considered himself the town's comedian, coming up with lame jokes, which he proudly thought up himself.

Irving smacked his lips and turned away trying to clear his mind from Bailey and his jokes. He heard a vicious swing and a curse and turned back to see the ball several feet from the tee. Irving tried to suppress a grin. Bailey's wife stood stone face while Irving's wife glared at her husband.

Bailey, red-faced set the ball back on the tee once again and proceeded to address the ball again, this time silently. With one mad eye on the ball, he swung furiously at it, praying to make contact. The foursome watched with relief as the ball soared down the fairway about seventy yards, half of that on several bounces. Bailey was relieved he made contact, but still frustrated he didn't even out distance Irving's wife.

Irving sat in the golf cart red-faced with laughter. Bailey, red-faced with embarrassment, moved off the tee area to let his wife hit her ball. After placing the wood behind the ball and trying to remember her lessons, she swung hard at the ball only to watch it slice toward the next fairway.

The ball barely missed another foursome as they ducked for cover. One obviously perturbed man shook his fist their way and yelled something they couldn't hear.

"What did they say?" asked Mrs. Bailey, straining to see who was yelling.

"Maybe I should go over and apologize," she added.

"No," Bailey said, more concern with his own shot then with the irate golfers. "Your turn Irv," he added.

Irving eyed him with confidence, then out of shear cockiness he grabbed a two iron out of the bag and began setting his ball up when Bailey broke in.

"It's over three hundred yards to the green. I think a wood would be better." There was a hint a panic in Baileys' voice. If he could hit it further with an iron than I could with a wood, then I would look bad, Bailey thought. To his surprise Irving eyeing him coldly, walked over to the cart and exchanged clubs, pulling out his driver.

Remembering the tips from the golf pro, Irving brought the club back slowly, almost deliberately. Sensing three pairs of eyes on him, he let out a sigh and dropped the club.

He closed his eyes and prayed he would make contact, brought his club back and swung at the ball with all his strength, which wasn't much anyway. He was horrified to discover that he completely missed it. Amid the chopping laughter of Bailey, he could make out the mechanical low-key voice of his wife.

"Keep your head down and keep your eye on the ball," she said in an almost scolding manner. "Remember what Mr. Woods said."

Without looking at her, Irving prepared the ball and swung again, this time with his eyes open, sending the ball down the fairway at least a hundred and fifty yards.

"Good shot dear," the mechanical voice said. Irving feeling a little better watched the shot bounce down the fairway. He turned and faced Bailey's puffed up reddened face. Bailey, sitting next to his wife in the cart, glared back at him.

Irving thought about chiding his neighbor then thought better of it and got into his own cart, where his wife waited, as she wanted to drive.

"Was that a nine or a ten on that last hole," she chirped. Irving glared at her as if she said an obscene word.

"An eight. You got the ten." Bailey at that moment darted off suddenly almost throwing his wife out of the cart. He raced the golf cart down the path as fast as it could go. His wife held onto her visor as if it was going ninety miles an hour rather than the fifteen it was really going. His wife thinking that highway rules applied badgered him to slow down.

"Harry. Really. Racing like some teenage hoodlum. You should be ashamed of yourself. Harry. Harry, you're not listening to me."

Bailey wasn't listening. He was looking back only to see Irving still parked next to the tee off area. Irving watched him smugly.

"Hurry up Irv. There's people coming up behind us and you know how I hate to be rushed," his wife said.

After a silent moment, he gently let off the brake and slowly eased the cart down the gentle slope to where Bailey had stopped next to his wife's ball.

She got out and with her club high above her head marched over to her ball. Bailey did the same but in the other direction. Irving watched the two hit their balls before he passed Bailey with a grin.

"Irving," his wife's tinny voice said, pointing back at the tee off area. "You passed my ball."

Irving stopped the cart with a jolt and glared at his wife who just looked helplessly. Turning backing to drop off his wife, he caught a glimpse of Bailey.

"Harry," said Mrs. Bailey. "He can't make a U-turn like that can he? Not unless it's posted. He's awfully lucky there isn't a police officer around."

She turned to her husband but he was in the middle of rolling his eyes.

****

"You owe me ten big ones," beamed Irving as he checked the scorecard again. "Yup. You shot an eighty and I shot a seventy-nine. So I win," he said slapping the card to dramatize the point.

"I don't have it on me right now," muttered Bailey more to himself. "You'll have to wait for the Social Security check which comes next week."

They stopped at an intersection, on the way home and waited for a Cadillac that was driving very slowly from their right. Bailey was driving while Irving sat next to him, his mind elsewhere. The two wives sat in back chattering softly.

Just as the other car entered the intersection, Bailey, losing his patience suddenly jack rabbited from their stopped position and passed right in front of the befuddled Cadillac, which had to stop suddenly. Irving could see the two horrified expressions of an elderly couple from his side.

"Damn those young punks," the white hair man mouthed, shaking his small bleached white fist at them. Irving could see the white hair lady putting her own gnarled hand on her husbands as if to calm him down.

****

"Calm down George. Or you will rip out your stitches."

"Damn my stitches. Someone should teach those young punks how to drive," the old man stammered. He wheezed once or twice as he stared after the car. He eased the Cadillac forward even more slowly this time and continued on their way.

"If you weren't going so fast, maybe this wouldn't have happened," scolded the old woman.

****

"Harry. You should drive more carefully," came the expected whine from the back seat. "You drive on the road almost as bad as you do on the golf course. You too, Irving. Gracious sakes. The two of you acting like kids..."

Irving and Bailey both closed their minds to the voice, each deep in his own thoughts.

Bailey was still thinking about the game, while Irving was remembering his long dead sister. Even though, it's been well over twelve years, he still grieves and when he is alone, he weeps silently for his sibling, who was five years older than he. She was more of a mother to him, since his own mother had passed away when he was young.

He had loved his sister as he loved no one else, even his wife. He loved his wife when they were younger and even that was a different kind of love, more of an infatuation that love. It was a physical love, a tolerable attraction that died many years ago. Little by little their marriage seeped away to almost nothing.

His sister's funeral was a nightmare for Irving. The ordeal put him in the hospital, where he had wished he would have joined her. They released him several days later and could not get any closer than ten feet from her grave.

When he got home from the funeral, he locked himself in his room and didn't see anyone for days, not even his wife. She waited patiently for him to leave his room. He recovered slowly and even now can't bring himself to talk about her to anyone.

"We're home," the voice said, bringing him out of his daze.

He had grown to almost detest that voice, feeling the cold hand on his shoulder. He didn't bother to acknowledge anyone as he made his way into his house briskly.

He undressed slowly and stepped under the hot shower, submerging his head under the steaming spray. It seemed to wash all the memories away. He heard that when one grows older and therefore nears death, one becomes more and more afraid of loneliness and naturally seeks other people. Irving had always been a loner, needing almost worshipping his time alone, despite the constant fear of death that has haunted him since his sister's death. He could feel it's cold presence even in the shower.

"What dear?" screeched his wife, her voice penetrating the roar of the shower.

"Nothing," screamed Irving, then. "I didn't say anything," he said leaning his head against the tile as he watched his hand shake. He felt a cold shiver shoot through him and he dunked his head under the spray as if to drown out all noise. He felt frustrated that she violated his privacy. His thoughts raced through his mind like a projector, slowing to slow motion.

It started with his wife, with whom he met in high school years ago. She was one of the popular girls while he was somewhat shy. She even looked a little like his sister and was happy when they got along so well.

His head was pounding now, like a jackhammer. He got out of the shower and shut the water off. After drying himself off, he got dressed in clothes that somehow appeared. Yet he gave no thought where they came from. He looked one last time in the mirror before he opened the door only to be greeted by his wife's voice. He saw that it was dark outside and sniffed at the familiar odor of dinner. It was the same odor from last night and the night before.

The little dog, her dog, nudged affectionately at his leg and wagged its tail wildly. It went into its begging routine. It didn't notice the sneer of its master as it was concentrating on the simple trick the human had taught it.

Irving's wife watched with worry as her husband went roughly by the dog and outside to sit on the patio.

He made his way down the deserted street unsure of his destination. He heard a dog bark somewhere. It was a deep barking that penetrated his mind. He passed the Nitdwits' home and could hear the constant yelling of two people who had the same temperament.

He remembered when they had invited him and his wife over for dinner. They would berate each other despite the company. It got to the point where everyone had some excuse from going over to the Nitdwits for dinner. Through the window he could see the silhouettes of the two facing each other in immortal combat.

Irving walked on, closing his mind to the voices, not of the Nitdwits, but of his wife's and even Baileys, echoing in his mind. He walked past the house of Leo and Rosetta Skinner, who were rarely ever seen in public, except the mornings when Rosetta could be seen driving slowly out of the driveway on her daily trips into town, where she worked as a volunteer. They were both in their nineties, white haired and hunched over. Their skin like that of crumbled up newspaper.

Irving couldn't remember when the last time he saw Leo Skinner. It was about two or three months ago. Odd for the fact that they lived less than a hundred yards away. As he passed the house, he saw no movement, nor was any lights on. It was almost seven and he guessed that they had gone to bed. The next house was vacant, yet it seemed more lived in than the Skinners.

He walked slowly deep in thought, until he came to the intersection, where he stopped and recollected where he was. He turned left and kept walking, until he came to an overpass that spanned the freeway out of the community. He studied the empty onramp and the mileage sign that told the mileage to the large city to the north. He thought of the last time he made a trip into town. They went with the Baileys and the Taylors in the El Dorado. It seated the six comfortable, despite having to stop at every gas station so Mrs. Taylor could use the rest room. The city was only thirty miles away, but it took an hour and a half.

Despite two wrong turns, three near collisions and two shaking fists and one memorable wrong way trip down a one-way road, they finally arrived at the major shopping center, which housed the large department stores.

Bert, who had been driving, was beginning to get his color and his breath back as they parked in the large parking lot.

They all got out of the car and stretched their legs as they stared at the local people as if they were aliens.

Young people clad in cutoff jeans and flip flops or sandals and highly decorated T-shirts walked by, along with young couples towing small children. Teenage kids on skateboards roared by, despite the sign banning them.

To the request of Baileys' wife, they made the pilgrimage to the usual restaurant, which specialized in unusual orders. The restaurant, which featured their employees dress in ridiculous red and white stripe uniforms who ushered customers to their seats or waited on tables. One annoying young man who ushered the six strangers to their table would bang on a small snare drum, which supposedly signaled the arrival of the newcomers. The drumming, which gave Irving a terrible headache, reminded him of Dick Nitdwits' voice.

When they had been seated, a young girl who wore a bright pink, candy stripe uniform smiled a colorful smile at them. She exposed multicolored teeth, each painted with alternating colors at them. In a loud high-pitched voice, she asked how they were doing and gave them weird menus and left them to their decisions.

Suddenly a loud police whistle shrieked through the restaurant, subduing the conversation and fueling Irving's headache even more.

"Let's go Irv. This place is full of weirdoes," begged his wife under her breathe.

She watched in bewilderment as two employees ran an empty stretcher between the tables. They stopped at a table and grabbing an unexpecting customer, playfully guided him onto the stretcher and carried him away, amid the laughter. Laughing they let him go and he rejoined his family, several shades redder.

The siren sounded again and another employee, this time dressed in a clown's outfit, ran in from the back and began throwing candy at children, who had their arms outstretched, pleading and giggling for more.

One piece of candy, off target, hit Bailey in the side of the head, knocking his glasses off. He glared at the clown who ran back from where it came. Bailey tried to say something but the siren went off again. Just as he was about to yelled something the siren stopped and all was quiet, which caught him yelling at his wife. Everyone looked at the six and especially at Bailey who stopped in mid scream. Forty pairs of eyes focused in on the six and they studied the surface of the table as if it held an important message. Irving couldn't stand it much longer and got up and stormed out followed by the other five.

"Can you believe that?" Irving said, waiting for them outside in the hot dry sun.

Bailey rubbed his temple as in after thought while the three wives babbled about the restaurant.

Irving remembered the episode from the overpass as he looked down on the almost empty freeway. He shivered as the cool night air swirled around him like a blanket. He shivered again and started back to his house and his wife and her idiot dog.

The End

Other Novels by Jim Seckler

Red Mirror
The Peregrinate Chronicles
Sweet Slice of Fear
Three Faces of Shame
GK-417
Revenge
Final Destination
Let the Chips Fall Where They Die
Witches Rum
Black Eagle – screenplay

ABOUT THE AUTHOR

Jim Seckler has written 14 novels, a novella and a screenplay. A former newspaper journalist, he currently resides in Arizona.